Heaven
Sent

VANESSA MILLER

WHITAKER
HOUSE

All Scripture quotations are taken from the King James Version of the Holy Bible.

HEAVEN SENT
My Soul to Keep ~ Book Three

Vanessa Miller
www.vanessamiller.com

ISBN: 978-1-62911-567-2
eBook ISBN: 978-1-62911-589-4
Printed in the United States of America
© 2015 by Vanessa Miller

Whitaker House
1030 Hunt Valley Circle
New Kensington, PA 15068
www.whitakerhouse.com

Library of Congress Cataloging-in-Publication Data

Miller, Vanessa.
  Heaven sent / Vanessa Miller.
     pages ; cm. — (My soul to keep ; book 3)
  ISBN 978-1-62911-567-2 (softcover : acid-free paper) — ISBN 978-1-62911-589-4 (ebook)
  1. Women—Violence against—Fiction. 2. Self-realization in women—Fiction. I. Title.
PS3613.I5623H44 2015
813'.6—dc23
                              2015021966

1 2 3 4 5 6 7 8 9 10 ⨆ 22 21 20 19 18 17 16 15

Prologue

Leah Davison's father and half brother had been hospitalized, and it was all her fault. Now that they were back home and resting, she decided it was time for her to fess up. Leah came into the room and sat down in a chair across from her mother and father. She put her hands over her stomach and leaned forward, biting her lip.

"Is something wrong, honey?" her father asked her. "You look so sad."

"I have to tell you something, Daddy, and I'm just worried that you're going to hate me after I tell you what I've done."

He sat up. "I could never hate my own flesh and blood. Why would you even think a thing like that?"

Tears were streaming down Leah's face as she said, "I did it. I paid Summer to accuse you of molesting her daughter." After she'd blurted out those words, her trickle of tears became a waterfall. "I'm so sorry. I'm so, so sorry for what I've done."

Other than Leah's crying, the room was silent for several beats before her mother asked, "Why would you do a thing like that?"

Leah lowered her head. "As Daddy's public relations manager, I have full access to his files at church. One day, I found a file marked 'Solomon Harris.' I wasn't familiar with the name, and I was curious." She started crying again, then looked up at her father. "You should have told us, Daddy. You and Mama had no right to keep that from us."

"I'm sorry that I let you down, Leah."

The moment those words were out of his mouth, her mother stood up, outraged. "Why in the world are you apologizing to her?" She turned to Leah. "Do you know what you've done? My husband almost died over that woman's allegations, and to discover that my own child had something to do with it…." Her voice caught as she started hyperventilating.

"Calm down, Alma," Leah's father said, his voice steady, gentle. "No sense in you having a heart attack and joining me on this sickbed."

"Please sit down, Aunt Alma," Larissa echoed. "Uncle David's right—you're getting way too worked up." She turned to Leah. "Can you just explain to everyone why you thought having this woman extort money from Uncle David was a good idea?"

"I'm sorry, Mama."

"You're sorry. Is that all you have to say for yourself?" Her mother took a few deep breaths as she tried to calm herself.

"I was just so mad," Leah responded. As her mother started to get up again, she quickly added, "But I may have overreacted."

"Even if discovering that you had a brother upset you, I don't see the need for extortion." Larissa stared at her, completely confused.

"This is a lot to take in right now. Can you help us understand what you were thinking?" Her father still spoke in a calm, even voice.

Leah pointed at Larissa. "Larissa and I are the same age. When it came time for me to go to college, you and Mama sat me down and told me that there wasn't enough money in the college fund for me to go to UCLA, my preferred college, and I accepted that because I knew that Adam was in college at that time, and that you would be footing the bill for Larissa's college expenses, as well."

"Your mother and I tried our best to save as much as we could for college, but we weren't earning as much in those days as we do now," her father tried to explain.

"Then how come Solomon was able to go to Harvard?" Leah demanded. "Why wasn't he told to scale back on his college dreams and be a good little team player like I was?"

"Your father had no say in Solomon's decision to go to Harvard, or any other school he might have chosen, for that matter," he mother said.

"I think you're allowing yourself to be deceived, Mama. Daddy practically has a siren to Solomon in that folder of his. And I'm willing to bet that you've never seen any of its contents."

Alma looked from her daughter to her husband. "What is she talking about, David?"

Sighing, Leah's father turned to Larissa. "Would you mind going to my office and getting that file on your way home from work tomorrow?"

"Mama doesn't have to wait another day," Leah piped up. "I can go get that file tonight and bring it back."

"No, you've done enough," her mother said. "I'll look at it tomorrow." With that, she got up and started for the door. Before leaving the room, she turned back to Leah. "I'd start looking for a new job, if I were you. Because I'm going to begin looking for a new public relations manager for the church first thing tomorrow."

Leah leaped out of her chair. "You can't fire me. I work for Dad and the church, not you."

"Your father is in no position to run that church, thanks to you and that woman you hired to spew all types of false allegations at him." She huffed, then took a deep breath and said, "Please clean out your desk. We'll give you two months' severance pay. That should give you enough time to find another job." With that, she left the room.

"Are you really going to let her do this to me, Daddy?" Leah pouted. "Where am I supposed to find another job on such short notice?"

Her father held out his arms. "Come here, Leah." When she stepped into his embrace, he hugged her, then told her, "Things will work out. Just give me some time to talk to your mother."

Pulling out of his arms, Leah asked, "Why do you have to talk to her about this? Why can't you just tell her to stay out of it? How can she just fire me like that?"

"What you did was wrong, Leah," Larissa put in. "Aunt Alma had every right to fire you."

Leah swung around, becoming hysterical. "You stay out of this, Larissa. All you've ever done is try to steal my father's affections from me. And now that I've admitted what I did, you just want to make yourself look good in Daddy's eyes. But he's not your father, and you need to remember that."

"He may not be my father, but he's the closest thing to a father that I've ever known."

David lifted a hand. "I'm not going to have the two of you arguing like you used to when you were kids. I thought this dispute had been settled a long time ago." He turned to Leah. "Your mother and I adopted Larissa when it was clear that her parents weren't coming back for her, so she is as much my daughter as you and Tamara are. I hope we are done with this conversation once and for all."

But Leah wasn't done. This family had mistreated her for the last time, and she was going to show them, once and for all, that she didn't need the Davison clan. She would succeed on her own.

1

Fashionable," "chic," and "stylish" were words normally associated with Leah Davison's sister, Tamara. But ever since Leah had signed on as an event planner with Stephen and Smith, she had upped her own game. Leah knew she would never be as beautiful as Tamara or her sister-in-law Larissa. But if the attention she'd been receiving from men lately was any indication, she looked pretty good. To top it off, her boss had recently commended her on the wonderful job she was doing and hinted at a coming promotion.

Leah's previous position had been the public relations manager for her father's church. She had loved that job, and the loss of it—admittedly her own fault—had landed her in the awkward position in which she now found herself.

Her latest event was a party at a nightclub where the liquor was flowing freely, and Ned Turner—a former client who was too handsome for his own good, and for the good of unsuspecting women—had had the audacity to strut into the club and crash the private party. Leah was tempted to ask security to show him the door, but she didn't want to draw attention to the uninvited guest—who, she was almost certain, had been stalking her. His presence could cost her that promotion. So, she just kept doing her job and prayed that he would go away.

Leah smiled as she handed her business card to a potential client. The guy was the CFO for one of the local banks, just like tonight's guest of honor, and he didn't look like the kind of man who spent his time worrying about how much things cost. Her favorite kind of client.

Then she noticed Ned inching his way toward her.

Leah excused herself, then ducked into the kitchen, hoping Ned wouldn't follow her there. Her pretext was checking on the meal preparations, so she stepped up to the chef. "How's everything going, Chef Darnel?"

"Everything is superb, Leah," he replied. "Now, what are you doing in here? You know I don't like lookie-loos in my kitchen."

Like most chefs she routinely contracted with, Darnel was extremely temperamental. That trait always got on her last nerve. But his hors d'oeuvres never failed to impress her clients, many of whom requested specific recipes for various dishes he had prepared. So, Leah lived with his moods. "I was just checking to see if you needed help with anything."

"What do you mean? You don't have enough to do that you need to scrounge for work in the kitchen?" He shooed her away. "Go see to your guests up front, and let me attend to my kitchen."

Leah wanted to object. After all, she was the one who had hired him, and figured that gave her the right to hide out in "his" kitchen. But Chef Darnel was not only known for his exquisite hors d'oeuvres; he had walked off numerous jobs screaming bloody murder for the smallest of infractions. And his contract allowed him to keep two-thirds of the contracted price, whether he acted like a fool or not. Leah decided not to mess with him. "All right," she conceded. "I'll just go on back out there and check on my client."

With her head lowered, Leah returned to the party, wondering how in the world she would manage to escape being noticed by Ned the stalker.

All her pondering came to an end as she crashed right into him. "I—I'm so sorry," she stammered, looking up to find him staring down at her.

"No need to apologize," he said with a smile. "I was looking for you."

"You were? Uh, why?"

Leah could have kicked herself. Ned was one of the first clients she'd worked with at Stephen and Smith. After she'd pulled off a successful event, Ned had called and asked her out. Leah had been flattered that such a handsome, accomplished man wanted to date her. He was the founder and president of a financial planning firm that was evidently doing very well. She'd gone out with him a few times, only to discover that he had a serious personality defect.

"You haven't returned any of my calls in over a month," he said, "so I'm trying to figure out what's wrong with you."

In Ned's world, nothing was ever wrong with him; it was always someone else, hence the personality defect. Leah didn't know why, but she got a bad feeling when she was close to Ned. It was like God was sending her signals, telling her to run. Leah glanced around the room, hoping to catch the eye of one of the security guards, but the closest one was all the way on the other side of the club.

Ned grabbed her arm. "Come sit with me. We need to talk this out."

She pulled free from his grasp. "There's nothing to talk about, Ned. I'm at work, and I would like for you to leave."

Smirking at her with those cold, dark eyes, he said, "I'm not leaving until you talk to me."

Leah felt trapped. "Okay, Ned. If you want to talk, then we'll talk. But give me a minute. I need to check with my client to see if he needs anything." She walked back toward the front of the room, where the party was in full gear. Her client was celebrating like there was no tomorrow. And if the drinks and well-wishes that had been floating around the club were any indication, his friends weren't ready for the party to end.

Tapping her client on the shoulder, Leah put on a happy face as she said, "Things seem to be going well."

"Oh, Leah, there you are. My buddy Ned was looking for you a moment ago."

"I saw him," she told him, then got right back to business. "I just wanted to see if you needed anything else."

He glanced around. "Nope. Everything's going smoothly. You weren't kidding when you said you knew how to throw a good party."

"It's my specialty." She looked over her shoulder at Ned, still stand-ing there, awaiting her return. Then she glanced at her watch. "Look, if you don't need anything else, why don't I just get out of here? I'll send in the cleanup crew in about an hour, and they'll clear everything out."

"That'll work," he said with a nod. "Just send the invoice to my office. Throw in some business cards, too. I have plenty of contacts I can hook you up with."

"Thanks. I really appreciate that." Leah backed away from her client, keeping an eye on Ned. She stood by the bar for a moment, pretending to be checking in with the bartender. The moment Ned took his eyes off her, Leah raced to the side door and ran as if a carjacker were trying to take her keys.

Unfortunately, she'd parked at the far end of the parking lot. By the time she made it to her car and grasped the door handle, Ned had run up behind her. "Get away from me!" she screamed, trying to open the door.

But he grabbed her by the shoulders and spun her around to face him. "All I wanted to do was talk to you, Leah."

"Leave me alone, Ned," she warned him. "I promise you, I will call the police if you don't stop bothering me."

"Oh, so now I'm bothering you? Funny, I wasn't bothering you when you were taking my money and eating for free."

"I didn't take your money. You paid my company, and I planned your event. But if I'd known then that you were a stalker, I never would have agreed to work with you." She'd never had these kinds of problems when she worked at the church.

"All you did was take my money," Ned snarled, his eyes taking on a crazed look. "You never wanted a relationship with me."

"Move out of my way, Ned." She tried to push past him to get to her car, but Ned was too strong for her. He lunged at her and proceeded to punish her bod with a series of blows. Leah cried out for help as he knocked her down to the ground and began kicking her. "Help! Please help me!" she screamed at the top of her lungs.

"No one's going to help you," he growled. "You're getting what you deserve."

As Leah faded into unconsciousness, all she remembered was Ned saying that she was getting what she deserved. And, in a way, she agreed with him. After all, it had been her conniving ways that had ultimately resulted in her father's heart attack. Maybe God was paying her back for the evil she had inflicted on her own family.

2

Looking herself over in the full-length mirror, Leah liked what she saw. It had been two months since the beating, and the bruises were almost entirely gone. Ned had been arrested. Now it was time to rebuild her life.

After getting out of the hospital, Leah quit her job at the event planning company. Promotion or not, having a job like that wasn't worth it if it meant she would run into psychopaths like Ned Turner. Since quitting, Leah had moved back to her childhood home, where she now lived with the father she'd once plotted to destroy and the mother who'd fired her for doing such a thing. But her parents were good people, and they had forgiven her without ever looking back once she'd confessed to her misdeeds.

Leah had been angry with her father after discovering that he'd had a son out of wedlock. At the time that she'd schemed against him, she had assumed that her mother knew nothing of his illegitimate son, and that her father had been cheating on her for the duration of their marriage. But Leah had been wrong. Alma Davison knew all about her stepbrother, Solomon Harris, and had even sent for him after her husband's heart attack. That was when the family had started the process of healing.

Now, after months of doubting herself, Leah was finally ready to reenter the workforce. She'd messed up her life by making so many wrong choices in the past, but this was a new day for her. A brand-new beginning.

"Looking good there, Ms. Davison," her mother said as Leah entered the kitchen.

Leah glanced down at her navy blue suit, then met her mother's gaze with a smile. "You're looking pretty good yourself, Mama."

Her mother handed her a glass of orange juice and a bagel smeared with vegetable cream cheese. "I figured you'd want something light to get you going."

"You're always so thoughtful." Leah kissed her on the cheek. "I haven't always been as thoughtful where you and Dad were concerned, so I'm especially grateful that you're so good to me."

"How could I not be? You're my own flesh and blood." Her mother hugged her. "I just wish you didn't have to start all over."

"Yeah. Me, too. But *que sera, sera,* right?"

"I used to believe that. Now I believe that what we pray for is what will be."

Leah didn't respond to that because she sure didn't believe it. She hadn't been able to pray since the night she'd been attacked and left for dead. Somehow, Leah felt that if God really had her best interests at heart, He never would have allowed her to run into Ned Turner in the first place.

"I know you don't believe me, but just know that I'm praying for you anyway," her mother said.

"Just make sure you center those prayers on my getting a job, and quick. I'm starting to feel like the underachiever in this family."

"I didn't raise no underachievers, so you hush your mouth with that kind of talk."

"Maybe you're just too blind with love for your children to know when one of them is a loser."

"O ye of little faith," her mother said as she kissed Leah's forehead. "Go get that job."

Leah got in her car and headed for her interview. She was meeting with an Internet mogul who'd met with instant success after starting a social media Web site called Pro-Site. It was like PayPal and Facebook rolled into one. Users could send videos of cats or messages about a person's humdrum life…or they could wheel and deal twenty-four hours a day. Anybody with a business wanted to be on this site. Consequently, advertisers also flocked there.

Pro-Site had grown so fast that it was now going public, and the company needed an assistant to keep one of the company's partners organized. If it wasn't so pathetic, Leah would have laughed at how her life was turning out. She had earned her MBA but was interviewing for a job that would include getting coffee for some bigwig.

Even though she wished she was excelling in her career like the rest of her family members, Leah wasn't going to cry over it. She was going to take her second chance by the horns and make the best of it.

Cory Parker was seated in the conference room with his executive staff, planning out the strategy for the most important IPO of his life. If all went well, the company would be worth billions, and he and his business partner would be able to walk away as multimillionaires. If all went really well, they would join the billionaires' club.

"Now, I know I don't have to explain to anyone in this room the importance of keeping closed lips on this," Cory said, scanning the other faces around the conference table. "Nothing we discuss here is to be repeated outside these walls."

Every head nodded.

"These next few months will make or break us. I'm going to need extreme dedication and lots of long nights. If you have vacation plans, scrap 'em. If we keep our heads down and work hard this next month, I promise you that after we've finalized this IPO, every day will feel like Christmas. Are you with me?"

"Of course," said Larry, his right-hand man. "I'm in it to win it. If that means going without a date for a while, I'm sure I'll survive."

"I have kids, so I may have to take work home from time to time," said Jasmine. "But I'm in, as well."

"Thanks, Jasmine," Cory said. "I appreciate your commitment to the company. I know how important your children are to you, and I promise I won't make you sacrifice your time with them for too long."

She nodded.

"Well then." Cory clasped his hands together. "Let's get to work."

Once his team had scattered, Cory went to his office and grabbed his mug. He was in for a long day and needed to fill up on the blackest, most caffeinated coffee he could find. He went into the break room and poured himself a tall cup, then took a couple sips before heading back down the hall toward his office.

He stopped in his tracks at the sight of a beautiful woman standing at his secretary's desk. For a second, he was afraid that fatigue had already set in, and she was only a mirage. But when he rubbed his eyes, he realized they weren't playing tricks on them. It really was Leah Davison standing there.

They'd been classmates in school and had attended the same church youth group growing up. And he'd had a crush on her for more years than he could count. He hadn't seen her since high school, and now she was standing five feet in front of him.

He'd almost worked up the nerve to ask her out in tenth grade, but then a girl he had been dating for all the wrong reasons had gotten jealous over his friendship with Leah and attacked her. After that, Leah had started dating his best friend, so Cory had contented himself with playing the field and quietly pining over the one woman he couldn't have. After graduation, they'd gone off to different colleges. Now they were all grown up, and Leah was just as beautiful as he remembered her.

But Cory was no longer that shy, gangly kid. He unbuttoned his jacket and puffed out his chest as he walked toward her. He now had muscles and biceps, and he certainly wasn't shy around the ladies anymore. He was determined not to be shaken and to remember who he'd become. "Leah Davison! What on earth are you doing here?"

She looked up at him. It took a moment, but recognition soon shone in her eyes. "Cory Parker. I thought the name was familiar when I was researching the company Web site, but I didn't imagine it could be the same person."

He smiled. "I moved back last year," he told her. "So, what brings you to our little company today?"

"I have an interview with Mr. Richards, but I think he must have forgotten about my appointment, because he's not here."

"You know how Dean gets when he's programming," Cory's secretary, Brandy, chimed in.

Cory turned back to Leah. "I apologize for my business partner. But, if memory serves me correctly, he was supposed to be interviewing for an assistant this week. I've been on him to hire someone to keep him organized. Believe me, he really needs the help."

"That's good, because I really need the job. If earning my MBA taught me nothing else, I've certainly learned a few organizational techniques that would benefit him."

Cory wondered why someone with Leah's credentials would be interviewing for an entry-level position. She should have years of experience by now. But he didn't want to pry, so he turned to Brandy. "Can you give Leah a tour of the office and then put her to work getting Dean organized?"

"But what if Mr. Richards doesn't want to hire me?" Leah asked.

"You worry about getting Dean organized. Let me worry about getting you hired."

As Brandy stood and led Leah down the hall, Cory mused that he no longer needed the coffee to get him going. His mind would be running a mile a minute with thoughts of Leah Davison.

3

I got the job!" Leah shouted as she came through the front door.

Her mother was in the kitchen, finishing the dinner preparations. She wiped her hands on a towel and rushed to greet her with a big hug. "That's wonderful, sweetheart," she said. "I never doubted you would, but it's fantastic news just the same."

"Thanks, Mama. I still can't believe it. But I kept telling myself that today was my new beginning, and look what happened."

"Look what God *made* happen."

Leah shook her head and sat down at the kitchen counter. "You can't credit God with this one. A former classmate of mine, Cory Parker, is one of the partners in the company. I haven't seen him in years. But the guy I was supposed to interview with today wasn't there, so Cory said that I could just have the job. I didn't even have to interview for it."

Her mother raised her eyebrows. "Sounds like the favor of God to me, sweetie. But let's not argue about that now. Just know how happy I am for you." She pointed toward the stove. "Help yourself to some dinner. I need to go upstairs and take care of something."

Leah watched as her mother left the kitchen. Then she stood quietly and peeked her head around the doorway to the hall. Her mother plodded wearily toward the staircase, looking downcast and dejected. What had happened to the happy woman she'd been just moments before?

She kept watching. Her mother climbed the stairs and went straight for her prayer room/office, which used to be Leah's brother Adam's bedroom. Once she had closed the door, Leah ascended the steps and stood just outside, listening in. She knew that her mother lamented her doubts about God, and she suspected that the woman was about to lay her case before Him yet again. Even though Leah was in no mood to acknowledge Him, she was curious about what her mother would say to Him in prayer.

Through the narrow opening in the door, she could see her mother down on her knees, head lowered, hands steepled in prayer. "Lord God," she began, "I thank You for all that You've done for my family. You've kept us safe from dangers seen and unseen, and I'm grateful for Your faithfulness. I know that it is in You that we live, move, and have our being; but Leah doesn't know that. She doesn't believe that she can trust You with her life. So, Lord, I'm asking that You would make that truth plain for her. Show Leah that You are not just my God but hers, as well. Bring her closer to You, and join her in relationship with Your Son, Jesus Christ.

"I thank You in advance for everything You are about to do for Leah, believing that You will perform Your word in her life. I believe it because You've already shown me that You are well able to bring all people to the knowledge of God, far better than I could ever dream of doing. I don't know just how You are going to work things out, but I trust You to do so. I'm calling on my Lord and Savior, Jesus Christ, and on a multitude of His angels to bring Leah into the kingdom. It's in Jesus' matchless name that I pray, amen."

Leah scurried back downstairs before her mother emerged from the room. She appreciated the thought, but she wasn't holding her breath for God to show up on her behalf.

When she returned to the kitchen, she found her father making himself a plate of pot roast.

"Hi, Daddy," she greeted him. "Guess what?"

"Well, hello, sweetie. And I couldn't possibly guess. Though, if I had to, I'd say you probably have some news about your job interview." He winked.

"I do." She beamed. "I got the job! I start tomorrow."

"That's wonderful, Leah." He gave her a warm hug. "I'm so proud of you. I know you'll do great."

Seconds later, Leah's mother entered the kitchen. "I didn't expect you home so early, David," she said, kissing her husband.

"I just got here. The church board meeting let out a little early."

"What about the minister of music? Were you able to convince him to stay?"

Leah's father shook his head. "No, but I'm not going to worry about it. The Lord sent him to us, and He will send us another. We didn't build our ministry on personalities, and we're not going to start doing that now."

"But, David. How will we manage in the meantime? His shoes will be hard to fill. The praise and worship has been so dynamic since he took over. I don't think our church can survive a return to those hymn-books." A shiver traveled down her spine that looked genuine to Leah. Apparently, her mother disliked the old church songs as much as she did.

"He gave us a two-week notice," her father said. "That should give us plenty of time to find a suitable interim worship leader until God shows us his replacement."

Her mother looked skeptical.

"Let's not worry about it right now." Her father grinned. "Did Leah tell you about her new job?"

"She sure did." Leah's mother made herself a plate, then sat down at the table with Leah and her father. After he'd given the blessing, Alma turned to Leah. "When does your new job start? Will you have to wait for them to do a background check?"

"Nope. Cory really got me the hookup," Leah said. "I'm in—no interview, no background check, no drug testing. He even gave me some work to do today, but tomorrow is my official start date. I'll be back there bright and early in the morning."

"You sound excited, sweetie," her father observed.

"I am, Daddy." Leah wiped her mouth with her napkin. "As recently as this morning, I was feeling down about the time I'd wasted, and also about the fact that I was applying for an entry-level position when I should be a manager or director by now. But then I ran into Cory Parker, and…." She shrugged. "All that didn't seem to matter anymore."

"Cory Parker…Cory Parker." Her father looked pensive for a moment. "Didn't you have a friend from youth group by that name?"

"That's right," her mother said. "I thought the name sounded familiar. You mentioned only that you went to school together."

Leah should've remembered that her father never forgot a thing. She hadn't mentioned the youth group connection to her mother because she knew she only would have called it proof that God was up to something.

"I guess I forgot about that," Leah mumbled. But the look her mother gave her told her she knew she'd withheld the information on purpose.

Just giving you something else to pray about, Leah mused.

The next morning, Leah finally met her elusive boss, Dean Richards. He looked anything but the picture of success that she had envisioned. His movements were awkward. His bifocal glasses didn't seem to help him at all when it came to finding the papers and drafts he needed in his messy office. And his wardrobe was just as unkempt as his desk. The man was the stereotypical genius who needed directions to his own home. Leah immediately understood why Cory had been so desperate for his business partner to hire an assistant.

His secretary, Brandy, informed her that Cory was especially nervous about Dean's lack of organization because some key paperwork for the IPO was missing. Leah's first assignment was to find it.

The office was a bigger disaster than any she'd seen. With countless stacks of boxes and folders piled on the desk, scattered on the floor, and clustered in the corners of the room, it would take her at least a week to create an orderly filing system and input the necessary information into the computer. Yet she refused to be daunted or discouraged. Leah was filled with a determination to do the best job she could. Cory was counting on her, and she wasn't going to let him down. She also wasn't going to let that MBA go to waste.

By the time Leah felt that she'd gotten at least a handle on her work, it was one in the afternoon, and her stomach was growling. Brandy must have heard it, because she popped in and said, "The graphics department ordered a bunch of pizzas for lunch. There are still a couple boxes in the break room, if you're hungry."

Leah thanked her, then hastened to the break room and washed her hands before grabbing a paper plate and a napkin. Then she opened one of the boxes—pepperoni and sausage. She was hungry, but not enough to eat meat on her pizza. She opened the next box, and then the next, until she finally found a plain cheese pizza. After putting a giant slice on her plate, she closed the box again and heated up her pizza in the nearby microwave.

"Don't tell me you still don't like pepperoni pizza."

She spun around and saw Cory leaning against the wall. "How long have you been in here?"

He grinned. "Long enough to watch you rummage through every pizza box. I'm glad you finally found one to your liking."

"The best pizza is the simplest." She removed her plate from the microwave and took a small bite. "How is it that you remembered, anyway?"

He was still leaning against the wall, studying her as if she were a Picasso. "I remember a lot about you." Then he stepped away from the wall and moved closer to Leah to add, "Like the fact that you and James Brooks were madly in love."

Leah rolled her eyes. "James Brooks was 'madly in love' with a lot of girls. He broke up with me the first week of college. Said he needed to explore his options."

Cory's nostrils flared. Shaking his head, he told her, "I wish I had known that he did that to you. I would have taken care of him."

Leah laughed. "I wouldn't have asked you to do that."

Cory lowered his head and looked into her eyes. "You don't think I could have taken him, do you?"

"I didn't say that." Leah grinned. "But you were a string bean of a basketball player who practiced dribbling in your free time. James was a football player and a wrestler who swung people around and knocked them down for fun. And he had about fifty pounds on you."

"Okay, maybe I wouldn't have been able to take him back then," Cory admitted. "But I've got a few muscles now." He flexed in front of her. "I might just go find him now and teach him a lesson about leaving a beautiful woman with a broken heart. You probably got terrible grades that first semester, right? Somebody has to pay for that."

She shook her head. "Straight *As* my first and second semester. I guess James didn't cause me that much heartache after all. He was all wrong for me, anyway." She shrugged. "I have a long history of picking the wrong guy."

"That's too bad," Cory told her. "I always thought you deserved the very best. I didn't think James wasn't the right guy for you, but I wasn't sure how to tell you."

"Is that so?" Leah raised her eyebrows. "You seemed pretty busy dating other girls to have been worried about me."

"Only because the one girl I wanted wasn't available. She was too busy wasting her time with a meathead."

Leah took another bite of her pizza, not sure what to say next. She couldn't say what she was thinking—that every inch of Cory Parker was divine. He was a chocolate-coated pretty boy with hazel eyes that seemed to draw her in. And that captivating smile of his was killer. However, Ned Turner had been handsome and pleasing to her eyes, as well. Her brother Adam had once told her that in a room full of good, she had a knack for finding bad. But this was a new day. She wasn't about to fall and bump her head again.

"I'd better get back to work," she said. "As you know, there's enough clutter in Dean's office to keep me occupied for a decade or so."

But Leah spent the next hour figuring out the telephone system. Brandy was leaving early for an appointment, and she needed Leah to take messages for both Dean and Cory during their afternoon meetings.

By four o'clock, Leah had taken several business calls for Cory, as well as two personal calls—one from Marlene, another from Nina— that left her feeling as if she'd made the right decision in backing away from Cory in the break room.

Cory's extension buzzed again.

"Pro-Site, Cory Parker's office. How may I help you?"

"Yes, is Cory in?" the female caller asked. "This is Tiffany."

"Mr. Parker is in a meeting right now," Leah told her. "Can I take a message?"

"Yes. Please tell him that I cleared my calendar, so I'll be able to make our date tomorrow night after all."

Yep, Leah thought as she hung up the phone. *You made the right decision this time, girl. Just keep dodging those bullets.*

For the rest of the day, she tried to put Cory the playboy, and all his women, out of her mind. By the time she packed up and left work for the day, she was feeling good about all that she had managed to accomplish. Cory would be happy to know that Dean was well on his way to being the picture of organization.

4

These days, Leah spent a lot of time with her family. She appreciated how the Davison clan had rallied around her in her time of need. They were constantly calling and inviting her to various events. This afternoon, the women were going to a local day spa for massages and pedicures, after which they had plans to meet the men at a restaurant for dinner.

They sat in the relaxation room wearing plush white terry-cloth robes and sipping iced herbal tea while they waited for their appointments. Leah leaned back in chair and exhaled. "I am so glad I was able to find a job so quickly. I sure wouldn't have been able to afford this massage if I hadn't, and my neck is so tense that I desperately need one."

"Girl, who you telling?" Larissa asked. "That son of mine is keeping me up so late at night, I can barely function. And that's not good for a doctor with patients who expect to receive quality care."

"Leave my godson alone," Leah told her. "He's perfect. Even if he likes to run around the house and break things."

"I plan to compensate for my sleep deprivation by taking a nap during my massage," Larissa told them.

"You're scaring me, Larissa," Tamara told her. "Jonathan is already dropping hints about starting a family. But if that means kissing a good night's sleep good-bye, he might have to wait a few more years."

"You'd better give me another grandbaby and stop being so self-ish," Alma teased Tamara. "Look at these bags under my eyes. Am I complaining?"

The girls laughed.

Then a masseuse came into the room and called Larissa's name.

She stood. "Time for my nap."

Leah's mother was the next to be called, leaving Leah and Tamara alone in the relaxation room. Tamara put down her magazine and turned to Leah. "How are you doing, really?"

Leah frowned. "What do you mean? Right now, or in general?"

"We're all enjoying ourselves right now. Mama always plans wonderful events."

"She does, doesn't she?" Leah smiled. "I used to imagine that I was like her...you know, moving behind the scenes, getting things done. Never needing anyone to pat her on the back. Just knowing that everyone else is happy is reward enough for her. That's why I became an event planner. I got a lot of enjoyment out of helping other people's visions become realities. But Ned stole that from me." Leah took a deep breath as tears formed in her eyes. "Some days, I'm fine. I don't even think about what happened. But, by the next day, something small will happen, and I'll feel as if I'm having a panic attack because I'm constantly watching my back when I walk to my car after work."

"I'm so sorry to hear that, Sis. I've been praying that you will forget everything about that awful man."

"I wish I could forget about him. I feel like that monster took away my life, and I'm desperately trying to get it back."

Tamara leaned over and hugged her sister. "Just remember one thing, Leah: Trouble doesn't last for always. One of these days, he'll be behind bars, and you won't have to think about him at all."

"When will that be? He keeps getting the trial date extended. I'm starting to suspect that he's got somebody on the inside of the court system working for him."

"It's time for Solomon to get involved," Tamara said. "At this point, you have to let go of your pride and tell the men in this family the truth about what happened to you."

Before Leah could respond to her sister, another masseuse stepped into the room and summoned her. But, unlike Larissa, who was no doubt already asleep, Leah would likely be too tense to enjoy the full effect of her massage because her mind was fully focused on what she had to do next.

She had to confess the whole truth to the men in her family, so that Solomon the attorney could get to work on her behalf.

They met the men at a posh restaurant in uptown Charlotte that Leah's mother had wanted to try because she'd heard that students from the local culinary institute would be preparing the meals that night.

"Let's just hope they can cook," Tamara muttered as they sat down at the table.

As if she could do more than fry an egg or toast a frozen waffle, Leah thought.

"There's no way the Merrimont would allow culinary students to cook our meal unless they were star students," Jonathan said.

Solomon rubbed his hands together. "All I know is, I'm starving. I don't care who cooks the food, because I'm about to bash."

"He's telling the truth," Larissa told the group. "Solomon even eats my cooking with a smile on his face. He must have a rock-hard stomach."

"Just like his old man," David said with a grin. He turned to Alma and added, "Of course, your meals are so good, I never have to rely on the spice of a hearty appetite."

Leah's mother grunted and eyed him as if she'd like to serve him up for dinner tonight.

Everybody laughed, Leah included. She was actually having a good time. There was only one problem: Adam was absent for yet another Davison family event. "Has anyone talked to Adam?" Leah asked the group.

"Adam isn't feeling well today," her mother said with a frown of concern. "He decided to stay at home with the kids. He wants to rest so he'll be well enough to speak to the youth group tomorrow night."

"Adam is making his own self sick," Tamara declared in her typical bold fashion. "You do realize that, don't you, Mama?"

Their mother nodded. "I've been praying for him."

"We've been praying for all of you," their father said, putting his hand over his wife's, "because we truly believe that God has a good life planned for each one of you. But you've got to grab ahold of it and refuse to let go."

"Amen. Preach, Daddy," Solomon said, clapping as if the bishop had just preached a soul-stirring message in church.

Once the first course had been served, their father David prayed over the food, and then everybody dug in. There were four courses in all: Caesar salad, cream of broccoli and cheddar soup, prime rib with garlic mashed potatoes, and, for dessert, the best banana bread pudding any of them had ever tasted.

When the server came back with the bill, their mother said, "You expect us to believe that our meal was prepared by amateur chefs?"

The server beamed. "They're talented, aren't they?"

"They shined like professional chefs," Alma affirmed. "I'd love to meet them, if at all possible."

"Let me check. I think the chefs were just finishing up, so they should have time to talk." The server went into the back and returned a few minutes later. "Good news. I can take you back now."

Alma stood. She looked around at her family. "Is anyone else coming?"

They all shook their heads.

"'This is all you," Tamara told her. "I'm so stuffed, I can't even move right now. We'll rest here until you get back."

"Suit yourselves. I just have to meet the chefs who cooked this meal."

As Leah watched her mother march off toward the back of the restaurant, she felt compelled to jump up and join her.

"Mama, wait up!" she called.

Her mother stopped and turned with a smile. "I'm glad somebody else is as curious as me. Though, I'll admit, I feel that I'm supposed to go back and meet the chef who made our meal. As if the Holy Spirit is prompting me because He has a bigger purpose for my being here." She winked at Leah. "Let's pray that He makes it clear."

They followed the server into the kitchen, where she stopped before a beautiful young woman with the most captivating eyes Leah had ever seen. Her mother looked equally transfixed, and Leah heard her mutter under her breath, "Honest and true."

"Chef Marla Williams," the server said to them, then turned to her. "These guests enjoyed your meal so much that they requested an audience with you."

As the server headed back to the dining area, Leah's mother extended her hand to Chef Marla. "I'm Alma Davison. And I simply had to let you know how thoroughly my family and I enjoyed the meal you prepared. None of us could believe that it had been made by someone still in culinary training."

"And I'm her daughter Leah. The food was definitely some of the best I've had in a while."

Chef Marla smiled from ear to ear. "Thank you so much for the compliments, ladies. Not only am I still a student, but I attend culinary school only part-time."

"You are kidding me!" Leah's mother said. "Someone who cooks as well as you should have her own restaurant, or be one of those celebrity chefs on television."

Chef Marla laughed. "I don't know if God has that plan in store for me. At this point, I consider my primary profession to be a ministry, and I'm not giving it up until He says it's time."

"And what is your primary profession?" Alma asked.

Leah only hoped her mother didn't offend the chef with her nosiness.

"I teach music at one of the local high schools," Marla said, "and I work privately with young aspiring singers on vocal performance."

"Is that so?" Alma asked, sounding intrigued. "Have you ever worked with gospel singers?"

Leah groaned inwardly. She was sure this woman was ready to call it a night, and here she was, getting grilled on her personal life.

But Marla nodded. "Gospel is actually my preference. I used to be the minister of music at my church back home, but they couldn't afford to pay me a regular salary, so I took a teaching job out here and started culinary school shortly after. I've been here about two years now."

"Is that so?"

Leah could see the gears turning in her mother's mind. Could almost hear her silently asking God, "Is she the one? Should we pursue her as a potential replacement for the minister of music?"

Alma asked Marla for her card before she and Leah returned to their table.

"This has been a wonderful day," Leah's mother said as the family prepared to leave. "We'll have to do this again real soon."

"Can we all head back to Mama and Daddy's house?" Leah asked the group. "There's something I want to discuss with all of you, but I didn't want to do it while we were out in public."

Her father searched her face for a moment. She smiled to cover her nervousness.

"I'll bring the car around," he said.

As he left the table, Leah's mother turned to her just as a shiver ran down her body.

"Are you sure about this, Leah?" she asked, her face serious.

Leah nodded. "I know I need help, and I won't get it until I stop hiding the truth from the whole family."

Solomon wrapped an arm around her shoulders. "We're here for you, Little Sis. Whatever it is, just know that Larissa and I have your back."

Leah smiled, grateful to have a half brother like Solomon. Her mother's relationship with him had gotten off to a rocky start, and no wonder, considering his birth had been the result of her father's infidelity with another woman. Granted, the affair had happened while Leah's parents had been separated—a mutual decision. But when they had reconciled, realizing that they couldn't live without each other, and he'd confessed that he had a child on the way, Alma had forgiven her husband—and hardened her heart against his unborn son.

Years later, when the truth had been made public, Alma had asked Solomon to forgive her for keeping him from knowing his father for so many years. After that, the two of them had forged a strong friendship.

Thank goodness for second chances. In Leah's family, those were not in short supply. She could only hope that they were ready to grant another, this time to her.

5

Once they were all at the house, Alma made a pot of coffee, along with several cups of tea for the non-coffee drinkers in the family, and they all sat around the dining room table, enjoying another piece of that scrumptious banana bread pudding, thanks to Chef Marla's generosity in sending them home with extra.

Soon it was time for Leah to take the floor.

"First, I want to thank you all for coming over to hear this. Solomon, Jonathan, I know how busy both of you are, so I'm not going to waste your time beating around the bush."

"What about me?" her father said. "I'm a busy man, too, you know."

Even though this was a serious moment for her, Leah appreciated her father's attempt to lighten the mood. "I know you're busy, Daddy. But you live here. So, you had no choice but to be here for me."

"I'll always be here for you, sweet pea." He winked.

Leah felt like crying. Her family truly loved her. She had been a fool, plotting and scheming as she had to expose her father's affair and his illegitimate son, especially since her mother had known about Solomon all along. If only she had gone to her father the second she'd found out about his indiscretion. Then everything would have been different. She wouldn't have lost her job at the church. She wouldn't have met Ned Turner.

"Thank you, Daddy." She rubbed her hands together, trying to stop them from shaking. "I need to confess something to you all, because I'm at my wit's end and need help.

"For starters, I need to apologize to the men in this family for keeping them in the dark as to all that happened, but I just couldn't bring myself to tell you until now. I did tell Mama and Tamara and Larissa, so I've had their support all along; but now, I really need everyone's support."

No one spoke. They all waited patiently, giving Leah the time she needed to get everything out.

"I told you guys that I had been attacked by a mugger and that I didn't know the man." She turned to Solomon. "You offered to help me with the case, to make sure things moved along as quickly as possible, but I didn't accept your offer because I didn't want to admit that I knew my attacker. In fact, I...I dated him."

"What?" Her father leaped out of his seat. "How long did he abuse you?"

She held up a hand. "It wasn't like that, Daddy. We went out only a couple times. But it didn't take long for me to figure out that he wasn't the one for me, so I suggested we stop seeing each other. It turns out that he disagreed, and that he doesn't take no for an answer. It's like he's possessed or something."

"Okay," Solomon said, taking charge. "Now we know what we're dealing with. Have you filed a restraining order yet?"

Leah looked away, ashamed. "No. I didn't want to have to explain why I was filing for a restraining order against someone I didn't even know."

"Well, now that we know the truth, you and I will go down to the courthouse on Monday morning and file the restraining order."

"Okay," she acquiesced. "But, Solomon, he keeps getting the trial date moved back. I don't understand how he's able to do that…or why."

"I'll check on that for you, too."

"Thanks. I just want to get this over with. I don't think I'll be able to get a good night's sleep until Ned Turner is finally put away."

"Did you say Ned Turner?" Jonathan asked, speaking for the first time since they'd gathered at the table.

Leah nodded somberly. "Do you know him?"

"He's been working on my company's investment strategy. He seemed like such a good guy. But I did feel uneasy when he was in my office one day and noticed the framed photo on my desk of the three of you," he said, pointing to Leah, Larissa, and Tamara in turn.

"Something is majorly wrong with him," Leah told him. "And if he knows I'm related to you, I wouldn't trust him with your finances."

"Oh, he is done," Tamara said, anger flaring in her eyes. "No husband of mine is going to keep the man who brutally attacked my sister on his payroll."

Jonathan put his hand over Tamara's. "I'll have my CFO move our accounts so that this madman no longer has access, and then I'll let him know that his services are no longer needed."

"Good," Leah said, folding her arms across her chest.

But the news she'd just received was a big blow to her system. How had Ned gotten so close to her without her knowing it?

First thing Monday morning, Leah went with Solomon to the courthouse and filed for a restraining order against Ned Turner. She was less than pleased, however, with the detective who'd been assigned to her case. They had first met each other while Leah had been recovering in the hospital.

Now, they met with him in a small conference room. After reviewing her file, the detective looked up with a frown. "I don't understand why you're asking for a restraining order at this time if you haven't heard from this guy."

"I can't sleep, I'm nervous all the time…he keeps delaying the trial, and he's now working for my brother-in-law," Leah explained.

"But you told us that you didn't know your attacker. Did he somehow track you because of the relationship with your brother-in-law?"

Leah shook her head. "Look, I'm sorry, but I wasn't telling the entire truth when you interviewed me in the hospital. My family was there, and I was too ashamed to admit that I had dated this man."

"So, you're saying you do know him?"

"Yes. We went out two or three times before I realized that he wasn't the one for me. But when I tried to break things off, he started showing up at different events where he knew I'd be. He attacked me at the last event I planned for my former employer."

"And now he's working for a family member?"

"Worked. Past tense," Solomon interjected. "Jonathan is planning to end his business relationship with Mr. Turner as early as today."

The detective looked Leah in the eye. "I'm glad that you finally came forward with the truth. I can't tell you how many women I've seen end up back in the hospital, or worse, simply because they were too embarrassed to offer the information that could protect them from future abuse."

After amending the police report, Leah filled out the paperwork for the restraining order.

As they left the courthouse, Solomon gave her a big hug. "I got your back, Sis," he reminded her. "You can stop worrying about Ned Turner. The judge will sign the temporary restraining order against him within two days."

"How temporary is this restraining order?" Leah asked, her panic rising once more.

"Calm down, Leah. Everything is a process, but we'll get through it. The temporary restraining order is valid for thirty days, because Ned has to be served and get his day in court. But you let me worry about court, because I'm going to make sure that he's hit with a restraining order that lasts at least five years. And after he is convicted and serves his time, we're going to ask for another restraining order."

Feeling overwhelmed, Leah went to work and was actually relieved to be tasked with the mindless job of delivering three cups of coffee and a tray of pastries to the conference room where Dean and Cory were working. She almost asked Brandy who the third cup of coffee was for, but she figured it wasn't her place. Plus, she was bound to find out when she made the delivery.

She knocked on the door, then slipped inside quietly and kept her gaze averted from the table, not wanting to interrupt the meeting. She set the coffees and pastries on an empty table near the wall, then turned to leave. On her way to the door, she stole a glance at Cory—and gasped when she saw Ned Turner seated next to him.

Leah bolted from the conference room and ran to seek refuge behind the nearest door in sight. It was a restroom—the men's, judging by the wall of urinals. No matter. She entered the stall farthest from the door and closed the latch to lock herself in. She tried to take deep breaths to keep herself from hyperventilating as tears of panic raced down her cheeks.

When she heard the restroom door swing open, she screamed.

"Leah?" Brandy asked. "Are you in here?"

She grabbed a wad of toilet paper and started wiping her face. "Y-yes, but I'm okay. Wrong door. Silly me," Leah hurriedly said, hoping that Brandy would just leave so she could regain her composure in private.

"Cory's worried about you," Brandy said. "He told me that you just ran out of the conference room as if the devil himself were after you. Are you sure you're okay?"

"I am," Leah lied, "but could you please ask Cory to come in here for a moment?"

"O-okay," Brandy said, sounding confused. "I'll get him right in."

Leah heard the door close. She took a fresh handful of toilet paper and continued drying her face. "Get yourself together, girl," she coached herself. "Just tell Cory that you quit, and then get out of here as fast as you can."

The restroom door swung open again. "Leah?" Cory said. "It's just me. Why don't you come out of there and tell me what's wrong?"

Leah undid the latch and pushed the stall door ajar, peeking out to make sure Cory was alone. Then she stepped out of the stall and tossed her spent tissues in the trash. "I want to apologize for the disturbance," she told him. "And I also wanted to let you know that this isn't going to work. I appreciate the opportunity, and I'm sorry to leave on such short notice. But my plan is to clean out my desk and be gone before lunchtime."

"Leah, Leah." Cory shook his head, clearly befuddled. "I don't understand. Can you please tell me what's going on? Why the sudden need to quit?"

She avoided his eyes. "Ned Turner." Just uttering his name caused a tremor of fear to course through her.

"Ned Turner? You know him? We brought him in to help us resolve some financial issues we need to iron out for the IPO."

She nodded mechanically. "That's why I need to go. I can't be anywhere near him."

Cory frowned. "I don't know what happened between you and Ned Turner, but I can assure you that you won't have to work with him. He's not an employee of this company, just a consultant."

"If he's a consultant, he'll be making routine visits to the office, and I...I really can't be around him." Leah was desperate to leave this place and run back home to the safe haven of her parents' home.

"We can work this out, Leah," Cory insisted. "I'll make sure that all our dealings with him happen over the phone or off-site. And our business will be settled in a month or so, anyway."

Leah found herself calming down. She liked working here. Brandy was nice, and Cory was wonderful. She hadn't figured Dean out just yet, but she didn't think he would be a terrible taskmaster. She could run now and find another job, but what if Ned showed up there, as well? Was she going to run from this man for the rest of her life?

"Thank you, Cory. I would really appreciate that." She managed a smile, grateful that he was willing to make concessions for her, and without demanding an explanation as to why she couldn't be around Ned. "You must think I'm crazy or something," she said with a nervous giggle.

"I think no such thing. Your happiness is important to me, and if that means keeping Ned Turner away from the office, then that's what we'll do. In fact, I'll go escort him out right now. This meeting can be concluded with a conference call later today."

"Thank you, Cory."

"Sure thing." Cory grinned. "Now, dry those tears and wash that face. I want to see that beautiful smile again." With that, he left the restroom.

As Leah cleaned herself up, she decided right then and there that she would never again cry over anything Ned Turner did to her.

6

Cory didn't know the details of Leah's beef with Ned Turner, but he didn't need to. The way she'd fled the conference room and then cowered in the bathroom was more than enough reason to honor her wishes where Ned was concerned. He strode back to the conference room, ready to show the man to the door. Anything to appease Leah.

"Did you figure out why my assistant went all crazy on us?" Dean asked Cory when he entered the room.

"She didn't go crazy, Dean. But I'm afraid that we'll have to ask Mr. Turner, here, to leave the premises and never come back. All future business dealings must be conducted elsewhere."

"What do you mean?" Ned demanded, rising to his feet.

"I mean just what I said. From now on, our consultations must occur over the phone, via video chat, or at an alternate location. If you aren't willing to work with us on our terms, we'll find someone else who is."

Ned turned to Dean. "And you're okay with this?"

Cory waited to see what his business partner would say.

"I'll defer to Cory on this one, Ned," he said with a shrug.

"Suit yourselves," Ned groused. He grabbed his briefcase and headed out the door.

"I hope you know what you're doing," Dean said to Cory. "I don't think we can afford to search for a new adviser right now. Not this close to filing, anyway."

"We won't have to," Cory said, confident. "He needs us as much as we need him. I'm certain he'll be amenable to the new situation."

Cory returned to his own office and tried to concentrate on the work he needed to do, but his mind kept replaying Leah's reaction to seeing Ned Turner. It was as if his presence made her fear for her very life.

He'd refrained from pressing Leah to tell him the reason for her negative reaction, but he knew better than to think that he could carry on without finding out the truth. Cory needed to get to the bottom of the matter. And, realizing he wouldn't get any work done until he did, he grabbed his keys and headed to Leah's cubicle to invite her out for a late lunch.

She initially declined, using the excuse that she had too much work to do. But Cory assured her that it could wait.

Then he turned to Brandy. "Can you handle the phones while we're gone?"

She smiled. "Yes, sir. I've got it covered."

"Are you sure you don't mind my taking a late lunch, Brandy?" Leah asked her. "I don't want to leave you alone to handle all the work."

Brandy waved her off. "I can take care of the phones, and you can finish the work on your desk tomorrow. But I think a break would do you good. Just go on with Cory and relax."

Cory read concern in Brandy's eyes, which made him all the more glad he'd decided to put his work on hold while he made sure Leah was okay.

"So, where are we going?" she asked as she grabbed her purse.

"It's up to you," Cory told her. "Do you have a taste for pizza? A burger? Or something else altogether?"

"I had a peanut butter and jelly sandwich at my desk a couple hours ago, so I could go for just about anything."

"Good," Cory said. "Let's go to Five Guys, then. I love their burgers."

"Ooh, I can feel the grease landing at the pit of my stomach already, but I love them, too," Leah said with a smile as they headed out the door.

Once they were seated with their burgers and fries in front of them, Leah glanced around the restaurant.

"You look nervous, Leah," Cory observed. "Are you all right?"

She met his gaze with a nod. "I was just making sure none of your women was here. I don't want to get my hair pulled in another catfight."

"That wasn't my fault," Cory told her, laughing at the memory. "That girl was crazy. I kept telling her that you and I weren't dating. You even had a boyfriend at the time. She just wouldn't listen."

"She couldn't stand the fact that you and I were friends. But Tamara and I set her straight. I bet that was the last time she pulled another girl's hair."

"I should tell your daddy about that," Cory said. "You church girls are dangerous. You're supposed to be all pious, praying for folks, but y'all are out brawling with the best of them."

"Hey, that girl asked for it." Leah was giggling now. "But, just so you know, Larissa made sure that we prayed for her at church that week."

"I remember Larissa—the cousin your parents ended up adopting, right? You used to call her the Goody Two-shoes of the family."

Leah stopped laughing. "I was horrible to Larissa," she admitted. "But, you know what I've come to discover? She's not so much a Goody Two-shoes as just good people. Larissa is the kind of friend you want in your corner. She's not going to tell you what you want to hear but what you need to hear."

Cory took a bite of his burger. "Oh, man. No matter how many times I come here, I can never get over how good their burgers taste."

"Remember when we thought going to McDonald's was a special day?" Leah started into her own sandwich with relish.

"This place is giving Mickey D's a fit."

"It's more expensive, but the superior quality is worth it to me. And to lots of people, apparently." Leah nodded at the line of customers, which now stretched to the door. They'd missed the lunch crowd, but the dinner rush was just beginning.

Cory popped a fry in his mouth. "Listen to us, talking about burgers and avoiding the subject we really need to discuss."

"I knew this free meal wasn't going to be free." Leah set down her burger, seeming to brace herself for whatever he was about to say.

"Don't be like that, Leah. I wouldn't be a friend if I wasn't concerned about you."

She huffed a sigh. "I have so many people who are concerned about me that I can barely breathe without someone in my family asking me if I'm okay."

"I don't want to smother you," he assured her. "I just want to make sure that you're okay—as your employer, and also as your friend. I haven't seen you in years, and I realize I don't know you that well, but it's also been years since I've seen someone as…unsettled as you were this afternoon." He tried to put it delicately. "Do you want to talk about it?"

She took a deep breath. "The reason I was so 'unsettled,' as you say, is because…because Ned Turner attacked me."

"What?" Cory nearly shouted. He looked around, embarrassed, then lowered his voice to add, "What do you mean, he attacked you?"

"I mean, he tried to force himself on me, and when I resisted, he beat me. We'd gone out a few times, and when I realized that it wasn't going to work out between us, I told him so. That's when things got really weird. He started calling me nonstop. Leaving messages demanding that I tell him why I no longer wanted to see him. Even following me—he'd show up just about any place I went. It really freaked me out. And then, when he made an appearance at an event I had planned with my former company, I tried to escape without his noticing me. That's when he lost it and attacked me."

Cory was completely alarmed. He didn't know what to say. All he knew was that Ned Turner had something wrong with him if he couldn't take no for an answer, and he certainly wasn't the type of person Cory wanted to work with. He only wished that he hadn't asked Dean to select the financial adviser for the IPO; otherwise, Cory could fire Ned without offending his business partner. He had already forced Dean to hire an assistant, and so, until the IPO was finished, Cory wanted to avoid ruffling any more feathers. But he was going to keep a close eye on Ned. If he made one wrong move, the man would be history, no matter what Dean might think.

"I'm so sorry," Cory finally said. "I can't even imagine how you must have felt, seeing Ned at the office today. No wonder you reacted so dramatically." He paused. "Have you filed a restraining order against him?"

Leah nodded. "I filed it just this morning. That's why I was late to work. I should have done it sooner, but I was too embarrassed about the situation to tell my family the truth, so I told them—and the police—that I had been mugged. He should be served with the order in the next day or two."

"Good." Cory nodded. "Since you have that in place, we can enforce the terms that I laid out for Ned today—that all future business dealings are to be taken care of away from our office."

"And for that, I'm speechless, Cory. I honestly don't know how to thank you—for honoring my wishes, and especially since you did so without knowing the details of the situation. I realize that Ned is this big financial wizard whose services you really need at this point; and for you to stand up for me, even in the face of that…I just don't know what to say."

Cory took her hand and gave it a reassuring squeeze. "You don't have to say anything. Just know that I'll always stand up for you."

7

After three weeks on the job, Leah had finally gotten Dean's office in order, but there were a few things that she hadn't been able to make sense of. Two of the items stood to threaten the upcoming initial public offering, so she tagged them with a note for Dean, telling him that she wanted to discuss them with him. So far, he hadn't responded to either one.

That afternoon, her cell phone rang. Leah didn't recognize the number. Usually, she would have let the call go to voice mail, but her curiosity got the better of her, and she answered.

"That restraining order isn't worth the paper it's written on," Ned snarled.

She dropped the phone as if it were a serpent. When she picked it up off the floor, she double-checked the caller ID. The number was definitely not the one she had stored in her contacts list as Ned's. She didn't know if he had borrowed someone else's phone, just so he could harass her, or if he had gotten a new phone after she'd blocked his number. But she didn't care. The courts had awarded her a five-year restraining order against Ned, and he couldn't come within three hundred yards of her. Leah didn't know why this man was so fixated on her, anyway. It wasn't as if they'd hit it off or anything.

She hit the "end" button on her cell phone, buried it in her purse, and got back to work.

"If Dean sees you answering your cell during work hours, he's going to have a fit," Brandy said, peeking over the wall of her cubicle. "His head is in the clouds most of the time, but he seems to have a radar for cell phones."

"Thanks for the reminder," Leah told her. "It won't happen again."

"You know I got your back, girl," Brandy said with a wink. "Next time you get an important call, just head to the break room or take the call in the restroom."

"Leah!" Dean hollered from his office, as he usually did whenever he needed her. But Leah wasn't complaining. She enjoyed her job, even if her boss was too lazy to walk out to speak with her, or even to use the phone.

"Must be his radar," Brandy said.

"I hope not. I actually like this job." Leah got up and went into Dean's office. As usual, he looked unkempt and out of sorts. "Did you sleep here again last night?" she asked him.

"I had to. We're about to take my new program live, and I have to get out all the bugs beforehand, or the IPO that Cory is working on will blow up in our faces."

"You're a busy man. I get it. But you still have to make time for yourself. You won't be any good to Cory or your family if you crash and burn."

Did he have a family? Leah knew next to nothing about his personal life.

He waved a hand dismissively in the air. "Yeah, yeah, I know. All work and no play…. But don't cry for me. I have plans for a weekend full of nothing but fun and sun."

"Good for you," she said.

She began to feel uneasy when Dean stared at her as if he wanted her to join in his "fun in the sun" weekend. It was an odd look on him, because she'd never pictured him as the type like Neil Patrick Harris's character on *How I Met Your Mother*. Dean was more like the role played by Jason Segel—the stable, dependable friend.

She cleared her throat. "What was it you called me in here for?"

"Oh, yeah. Back to business." He clasped his hands and stood up. "I can't find the developer file."

Leah went over to the file cabinet she'd purchased for his office. She opened the third drawer down, pulled out the file he was looking for, and handed it to him. "Did you need anything else?"

"You put a lot of my files on the computer, right?"

"Yes, sir. I thought you'd be able to keep up with the documents you needed if they were just a click away."

"That was smart thinking. But I can't find any of the documents on my computer. Can you show me where they are?"

Leah almost laughed. Dean was a computer geek. He was an expert at programming Web pages and working with graphics, but he couldn't find a simple document. That was funny. "You didn't have the proper software on your computer, so I installed it. May I?" She nodded at his computer.

"Of course."

Stepping behind his desk, she pointed at the screen. "See that little icon of a blue jar with the quill across it?"

He nodded.

"Click on it."

When he did, Leah showed him how to access his files. Then she stepped back around to the front of the desk.

"I don't know how I ever got along without you," Dean said. "Thanks for all the time and energy you've expended to get me organized."

"You're welcome. Did you get a chance to look at those two documents I flagged?"

He shook his head. "My mind is so jumbled with this new program that I can't wrap my brain around anything else right now."

"Those documents seemed important," Leah persisted. "Would you rather I discuss them with Cory?"

"I don't need you running to Cory behind my back," Dean said curtly. "I'll review the documents first chance I get."

"Okay." She turned toward the door.

"Sorry for snapping," Dean added with a sigh. "I'm just really busy and really stressed right now."

She pivoted on her heel. "I understand, sir. Please don't worry about it."

He collapsed into his chair and studied her for a moment. "What are you doing this weekend?"

"Excuse me?"

"The executive staff of Pro-Site has scheduled a retreat to the Bahamas to celebrate the release of Pro-Site Two. I think you should join us."

She'd heard all about the retreat—Brandy had been talking about it almost nonstop since her first day on the job. But she'd assumed that she hadn't made enough of a contribution to earn a spot on the trip. "Thanks for offering, Dean. With such short notice, though, I don't think I could swing it."

"Well, think about it, anyway. You could share a hotel room with Brandy."

"I don't get it. Why are you offering me this opportunity? I haven't done anything but organize your paperwork. That hardly seems enough to warrant a trip to the Bahamas."

"That's what you think. But if you hadn't gotten me organized, I wouldn't have been able to bring the programming in on time."

"Well, I appreciate your noticing the work I've done." She hesitated, then said, "Let me think about it. I'll let you know." Walking out of the room, Leah was still trying to figure out what had just happened. At first, she'd thought that Dean was coming on to her. But since he'd suggested she share a room with Brandy, she figured he was probably just trying to show his appreciation for the work she'd done.

As she got back to work, the phone on her desk rang. As soon as she picked up, she wished that she hadn't.

"How is your day going?" Ned asked.

"Why are you calling me here?"

"Why shouldn't I call you there? I want to prove to you how much I've changed. I want us to get back together."

"That will never happen." She slammed down the receiver.

When the phone started ringing again, Leah covered her face with her hands. Frustration was setting in. She'd gotten the restraining order, and Ned had received it, but he just wouldn't quit. He wasn't going to leave her alone.

"You want me to get that?" Brandy asked.

"Please."

Brandy brought the phone to her ear and listened for a moment. "This isn't Leah," she said. "And if you call here even one more time, I will notify the police. Got it?" Then she clicked the receiver back in its cradle.

"What did he say?" Leah asked.

Brandy frowned. "He said that you need to watch your back."

Blowing out a sigh, Leah confessed, "I don't know what to do."

"Call the police. Report him for harassment."

"I've already filed a restraining order against him. You see what he thinks of that."

Brandy shook her head. "This is why I don't date a man unless he's saved for real and loves Jesus more than he loves me. And then, if we break up, I just tell him to go pray about it and to ask the Lord to find that perfect woman He has picked out for him."

"That's a good way to say, 'Buzz off,'" Leah said with a grin. "But Ned wouldn't bite that bait. I'm almost convinced he's the devil incarnate. At the very least, he's not going to pray about anything."

"It sounds like you really got one. I'll be praying for you," Brandy offered.

With all these people praying for her, Leah wondered why her life kept going from bad to worse.

Shortly after Brandy left her desk to take lunch in the break room, the phone rang. Leah was in a mood, so she was tempted not to answer. But it wasn't as if she was at home and could just ignore every call.

She picked up. "Pro-Site, Mr. Parker's office. How can I help you?"

"Why are you always answering Cory's phone?" the woman barked. "Where's Brandy?"

Leah held the phone away from her ear and stared at it for a moment. *You need this job*, she reminded herself before bringing it to her ear once again. "Brandy is on break at this moment," she said, as politely as possible. "Is there something I can help you with?"

"Yes," the woman hissed. "You can tell Cory not to be late for our date."

"And you are…?" Leah asked as sweetly as she could.

"You know who this is. Better yet, just put me through to his line, and I'll tell him myself."

"I'll put you right through." Leah quickly transferred the call and didn't wait for Cory to pick up. If he wasn't in his office, the call would just go to his voice mail.

Yes, she did know to whom she had been speaking. And what Cory saw in that Tiffany woman was beyond her understanding.

⌒

Approaching Leah's cubicle, Cory overheard her side of the phone conversation and couldn't help but be shocked by her malicious tone. Did she talk to all the callers that way? Or was it another unstable man calling to harass her? Either way, it wasn't a productive use of her time.

He'd believed her when she told him that the abuse she'd suffered at the hand of Ned had been a onetime thing and that it had caught her completely by surprise. He'd never once thought that she made a practice of dating abusive men.

She was too independent and too confident for that. Back in high school, Leah had always gone her own way and done her own thing. She was nothing like his sister, Lisa. The world was filled with women like Lisa.

He'd once witnessed a man dragging a woman by her hair into oncoming traffic. Cory and a few other bystanders had jumped out of their cars and pulled the man off her. The man told all of them to back off and then barked at his woman to "come on and get in the car."

Baffled, Cory had watched the woman's shoulders go slack and her head lower as she followed her abuser to his car. That, to him, had been the picture of insecurity: a woman who thought she was nothing without a man. Whether that man was good for her didn't matter; she just needed a man to help her feel worthy as a human being.

Cory was now feeling a burden for Leah like the one he'd felt the day he'd jumped out of his car to help a woman whose name he didn't even know. But he also had a burden for the rest of his employees. So, when he heard Leah hang up the phone, he walked up to her cubicle and peeked over the wall. "Hey. I was wondering if I could take you to dinner tonight so we could discuss something."

Leah shook her head. "I wouldn't want to keep you away from Tiffany."

Cory frowned. "What about Tiffany?"

Leah smirked. "She called to confirm your date tonight."

"Well, yeah, there's a movie she wants to see. But I have time for a quick dinner with you, because we need to talk about some things."

"I already have dinner plans for this evening," Leah told him. "Why can't we just discuss whatever it is right now?"

"You seem angry," Cory observed. "Have I done something to upset you?"

"I'm not angry." Leah fished her car keys out of her purse. "Look, Cory, this has not been a good day for me. I'm taking it out on you, and I have no right to do that. I'm sorry, but I need to get out of here so I can clear my head."

If he was being harassed at work, Cory doubted he'd be having a good day, either. "We don't have to do dinner, but I need to talk with you about the harassing phone calls you've been getting. I want to come up with a way to put a stop to them, so that they aren't causing you to lose your focus or taking up time you should be spending on other things."

"That was just Ned," she growled. "He must have just been served with the restraining order, and he was calling to tell me that it didn't mean anything to him."

Cory felt a wave of rage rise up within him. "He's done," he declared. "I'm firing him right now."

"You can't do that," Leah protested. "You and Dean have too much riding on this deal."

"There are a thousand consultants who can help us with this IPO. I don't need anyone hanging around this company, harassing the women I employ. That's a lawsuit waiting to happen. I've already met with another consultant, just in case, and he's waiting in the wings."

"Please think about this, Cory. My issues aren't important enough to cause trouble like that for your company."

It was true that Cory was in the middle of the biggest deal of his life and didn't want to do anything to upset the process. Which was why he'd continued working with Ned, even after discovering that he was an abuser. The way Leah had explained it, Cory figured it could have been a onetime incident that caused the man to lose it. He hoped that wasn't his general character. But if he was still harassing Leah, then Ned wasn't new to this. He was a creep, and Cory wanted no part with him.

"It's done," he stated. "I'm beefing up security in the lobby of our building starting tomorrow. And if Ned calls again, you need to inform me immediately. I'll call the police myself."

"You would do all that for me?"

"In a heartbeat," he told her. Then he walked away, pulling his cell phone out of his pocket. What Cory didn't say was that he was also striking a blow for his sister against the abusive husband who had beaten her to death on her twenty-second birthday. Cory had been only thirteen at the time, but he would never forget how devastated his mother and father had been to receive the news that their beloved daughter had been killed.

Lisa was the reason Cory had started attending youth group at Leah's church in the first place. He'd never told anyone about his sorrows. But, at that time in his life, he'd desperately needed God's love and guidance. Even though Leah hadn't known what her friendship had meant to him at the time, Cory knew.

And he was determined not to let her suffer the same fate as his sister.

8

Leah was meeting Solomon and Larissa for dinner at the couple's favorite Mexican restaurant. They took pity on her from time to time and allowed her to tag along. Even though Leah had gotten much closer to Larissa and had come to truly love her half brother, she still felt like a third wheel when she was out with the lovebirds. It was even worse when she went out with Tamara and Jonathan. Those two didn't have kids yet, so they were still all over each other like high schoolers in love.

But she couldn't concern herself with all the lovebirds in her family, because she was still reeling from her latest conversation with Cory. She'd almost thought he was asking her out. Why on earth would a man like Cory want anything to do with someone like her? She was so messed up, she might as well be a member of the Kardashian family.

She got out of her car and started across the parking lot, humming the tune of Kirk Franklin's "Brighter Day." Her mother loved that song, and Leah was singing it in hopes of making the lyrics a reality in her life.

But then she heard Ned's voice as he came up behind her. "Who are you meeting here? That lover boy from work?"

Leah swung around to face her enemy. "Leave me alone, Ned. Do you hear me? I don't owe you any explanations."

"Sure, you do. You're the one who got me fired, after all."

"I didn't get you fired. That was the result of your own actions. If you would have just left me alone, you wouldn't have any problems."

"Oh, really?" Ned sneered, his voice dripping venom. "And I guess it was my own actions that somehow made your brother-in-law decide he no longer needed my services. You had nothing to do with that one, either, right?"

Leah didn't respond. Nothing she said would matter to Ned. He was living in a world that he alone understood. She just wanted to get as far away from him as possible.

She tried to sidestep him, but he jumped in front of her. "Walk away from me while I'm talking to you, and I'll make you regret it."

Her upper lip curled with disgust as she considered the monster standing before her. He had filled her with so much fear and worry that she didn't know if she'd ever be able to shake it off. But she was tired of doing nothing while he did everything he could think of to her. She opened her purse and started searching through it.

"What are you looking for?" he snickered. "That meaningless scrap of paper the court gave you?"

He wasn't going to make her feel powerless anymore. She was done with that. Leah grasped the canister of pepper spray she'd purchased just a few days ago.

"What are you going to do, throw the paper at me?" Ned taunted her.

She was just about to blast him when she heard Solomon shout, "Get away from my sister!" He rushed over to them, grabbed Ned by the collar, and shoved him against the building. "Stay away from her. Do you hear me? Or I swear before God that I will come after you."

"Let him go, Solomon," Leah said, not wanting him to get in trouble for assault. "He's not worth it."

Solomon jabbed his elbow against Ned's throat. "You like to harass women. You want to terrorize somebody? Why not terrorize me? Come on, big man."

Leah pulled at Solomon's arm. "Don't do this."

Solomon released the pressure from Ned's neck and backed away. "It ends today. Right here and now. Or I will deal with you."

Ned rubbed his neck and coughed a few times. "Are you threatening me?" he wheezed.

"I'm stating a fact and making a promise." Solomon took hold of Leah's arm. "Don't you ever come near my family again." With that, he escorted her inside, leaving Ned on the outside looking in.

"Is he still out there?" Larissa asked when they sat down at the table.

"He'd better not be." Solomon was steaming. It almost looked as if smoke might start billowing out from his nostrils.

"Calm down, Solomon," Leah pleaded. "I don't need you getting mixed up in this craziness with Ned. I messed up. I knew I shouldn't go out with him in the first place, but I ignored the sense of foreboding because I was feeling lonely."

"We've all been there, Leah," Larissa told her with a nod. "Before Solomon came into my life, I doubted that the husband God had for me would ever show his face. Don't be so hard on yourself."

"I hear what you're saying," Leah told her, "but I still should have known better. Ned doesn't attend church. And he got so drunk the night of the party I planned for him that I had to arrange transportation home for him."

"Do you remember what your dad used to tell us all when we were teenagers?" Larissa asked.

Leah shook her head. He'd told them so many things, she could only guess what Larissa was going to say.

"I realize that he passed along many tidbits of wisdom, but one of his statements, in particular, stuck out to me." Larissa leaned forward in her seat. "He told us that sin is never polite. It won't just take you so far and then ask, 'Pretty please, can I take you a little further?' Once you open the door to sin, it will drag you as far away from God as it can take you."

Leah nodded, remembering. "And once sin has had its way, I'll be left to bear the guilt and shame of everything I did," she said, wrapping up one of his infamous sermonettes. "He was right. I've been so ashamed and filled with guilt that I let myself become a victim."

"Well, you're not a victim anymore," Solomon told her. "You've taken the steps toward putting that animal where he belongs." Picking up his menu, he added, "I'm not going to give that man another thought tonight. I say, let's order some good food and enjoy some good company."

Leah and Larissa picked up their menus, as well. Immediately after they had placed their orders, two police officers approached their table. "Solomon Harris?" the taller one said to Solomon.

"That's me," Solomon said. "Can I help you?"

"Sir, I'll need for you to stand up, turn around, and put your hands behind your back."

"What's going on?" Leah demanded. She jumped up, ready to defend her half brother from the big bad policemen.

"Step back, ma'am. He's being arrested for battery."

"I didn't batter that little twerp," Solomon insisted, rising to his feet. "I should have, but I didn't."

"My husband isn't a batterer," Larissa declared as she stood. "Uncuff him."

"Larissa, baby, you and Leah sit back down and let the officers do what they have to do," Solomon told her. "Don't get in the way. This will all be resolved in no time, I'm sure."

"I have a restraining order against Ned Turner, and my brother was just defending me," Leah told the officers. "He wasn't supposed to be anywhere near me. Why aren't you arresting him instead of my brother?"

"We saw the marks on his neck, so we have to take Mr. Harris in," one of the officers explained.

"But he's been stalking me. Don't you care about that?" Leah was screaming now. She couldn't fathom the injustice of it all.

"Hey, we're just doing our job," the other officer said. "Please step back, ma'am."

Solomon turned to Leah. "Do what they say. Eat some dinner. And then, when you're done, you and Larissa come down to the jail and bail me out."

"This is a nightmare, and it's all my fault," Leah lamented as she and Larissa watched the officers escort Solomon out of the restaurant.

Larissa huffed. "Stop blaming yourself, Leah. This isn't your fault; it's Ned's. I won't allow you to carry the blame that belongs to someone else. Now, let's try to enjoy our dinner. Then we'll go down to the jail and get my husband released."

"Okay," Leah finally agreed, even though her appetite was completely gone.

She picked at the complimentary chips and dip while Larissa polished off a plate of enchiladas. Then, they went to their cars and headed for the police station. It was a good thing Larissa was leading the way, or Leah probably would have gotten a speeding ticket.

Her life was in a shambles. She wanted to pull over and have a breakdown on the side of the road. But she had to hold it together so she could be there for Larissa and Solomon.

She could go ahead and have that breakdown once they were through dealing with this nightmare she had caused them.

After Larissa paid the bond, they still waited two hours for Solomon's release. It pained Leah to think of Solomon behind bars because of something she had done. Her family was going to turn her out if she kept bringing drama to their doorstep.

When Solomon was finally released, he hugged Leah and then kissed his wife. "Thanks for bailing me out, baby."

"Anytime," Larissa said with a grin. "Let's just not make it a weekly occurrence, okay? We don't want to blow our baby's college fund before he or she is even born."

Leah didn't understand how they could make light of such a dire situation. But, in the midst of her despair, she couldn't help laughing at their antics. "After all that's happened tonight, I can't believe the two of you are still able to make jokes."

Larissa put her arm around Leah's shoulder as they walked out of the precinct. "We might as well laugh. We certainly don't want to give that awful Ned the satisfaction of seeing us cry, right?"

"I guess you're right. But, to be honest, I've wondered if my having a breakdown in front of him might get him to have enough pity to leave me alone." She scratched her head. "I just wish all the crazy men came with a warning sign on top of their heads, so that, no matter how gorgeous they were, women would know to just walk away."

"Instead of talking about breakdowns, let's talk about breaking bread," Solomon said. "I'm starving."

"Y'all go on and spend some quality time together," Leah told him. Her appetite was beginning to return, but she was no longer feeling sociable. "I'm going home to get some rest."

"Can I give you some advice?" Larissa asked.

"Why not?" Leah asked with a sigh. "I'm getting advice from everywhere else."

"Don't just go home and sleep. Pray first and ask God for direction. Solomon and I will be praying for you, too."

Leah kissed them both before climbing into her car and driving off. She would leave the praying to them. Once she got home, she went upstairs and flung herself across the bed. The day had drained her of every ounce of strength. But every time she shut her eyes, she saw Ned beating the life out of her. Around three in the morning, when she was tired of trying to turn off the drama in her head, she turned on the television and surfed through the channels, seeking to replace it with some real drama.

It came as no surprise that there was nothing much of note on TV at this time of day. But she did come across an episode of a show she'd seen before. It was about a bipolar mess of a woman who couldn't deal with the fact that her boyfriend was tired of her abuse. After harassing him for months, she'd finally driven to his job and shot him in the face, right in front of his coworkers. The man had survived, but his face was a bit disfigured, and his eye twitched as he spoke of the horrible ordeal.

Ned had abused her after discovering that she no longer wanted to date him. Now he was taking pleasure in tormenting her and her family. She was so tired of being afraid of what lurked behind every corner. Tired of living her life as a victim. But what could she do? Just as sin didn't ask for permission, bullies never asked if it was okay for them to ruin a life.

⌒

"So, the prototype of the new Web site is ready, and now you're running off to the Bahamas to celebrate. I am completely jealous."

Cory smiled at Tiffany, not sure how to respond, since he hadn't heard everything she'd just said. He'd been lost in thought about Leah, wondering just how much abuse she had suffered at the hand of Ned Turner. He was also wondering how that parasite had weaseled his way into a job assignment with their company.

"You're distracted," Tiffany observed. "You barely watched the movie, and you've hardly touched your food. I know you've got a lot going on at work, but it's okay to relax a little. You're at the finish line."

"We aren't at the finish line just yet. My account executives are still working."

"Your account executives are about to embark on an all-expenses-paid trip. They should be burning the midnight oil with no complaints."

"I still feel a bit guilty about being out with you tonight," Cory admitted. "They've put their lives on hold for the past several weeks—months, even—and here I am, out for dinner and a movie."

"There's nothing to feel guilty about, Cory. You've cancelled every date we had scheduled in the last month. If you had bailed on me again tonight, I would have finally taken the hint and deleted your number from my contacts list," Tiffany said with a laugh.

Cory put his fork down and studied her. She was beautiful, well-educated, and successful. And he enjoyed being with her, but not enough to take their relationship any further. He would be doing her a disservice to allow her to continue hoping that they would become a couple. He decided he had led her on for too long already.

"Tiffany, I think we need to talk."

"I thought that's what we were doing." She was still smiling.

"No, I mean about us." He wiped his mouth with his napkin. "See, I don't want you to sit around waiting on me. There's so much going on in my life right now that I don't know if I even have time for a relationship."

She put her hands on the table and straightened her back. "It would be an understatement to say that this has caught me off guard, Cory. I thought we were having a good time together."

"I do enjoy being with you. I just don't know if this is the right time for us."

"Can I ask you something?" Tiffany's tone was calm and businesslike.

"Of course. What do you want to know?"

"Does your sudden desire to call it quits have anything to do with your new assistant?"

"My new assistant?" He frowned. "I don't have a new assistant. Brandy's worked for me for years."

Tiffany scowled. "Brandy isn't the girl who's answered the phone the past few times I've called you at your office."

"Oh, you're talking about Leah. She works for Dean."

"It really doesn't matter who she works for. Every time I have spoken to her, I've gotten the distinct impression that she's ticked off or something. And I ask myself why on earth you would let a person with an attitude like that answer your phone. But then, maybe she doesn't have the same attitude with your business associates."

"This is the first complaint I've received about Leah's telephone conduct," Cory admitted. "I'll speak to her about it first thing in the morning."

"Don't bother. The person I want you to speak to is yourself. We've got something. Don't mess it up." She put her hand over his and added, "We could be good together, Cory. Just give us a chance."

9

On Friday morning, as Leah was getting into her car to head to the office, she noticed a piece of paper tucked beneath one of her windshield wipers. She surveyed the area to make sure she didn't see Ned hiding behind a bush, preparing to jump out and attack her. Nothing in the neighborhood looked amiss, so she grabbed the sheet of paper, got in the car, and quickly closed the door, locking herself in.

She unfolded the paper and found a handwritten note from Ned:

I'm sorry, Leah. I will drop the charges against your brother if you agree to have breakfast with me today.

Crumpling the note, Leah decided that it was time for a conversation with Ned. She needed to get it through his thick head that they would never be a couple again—not that they had ever really been one. She pulled her cell phone out of her purse and called him.

"You got my note?" Ned asked, his voice calm and gentle.

That was the way he used to talk before he attacked her. Leah wasn't about to fall for it again. *Fool me once, shame on you. Fool me twice, shame on me.*

"Yes, I got your note, and I called to remind you about the restraining order."

"Oh, that little piece of paper? Don't worry about it. The police won't enforce it if you don't call and report me."

She sucked in a deep breath, then exhaled forcefully. "What do you want from me, Ned? Why don't we just get to the bottom of all this and then go our separate ways?"

"You sound so cold. Not at all like the Leah I know and love."

"You can't be in love with me, Ned. You barely know me. We went out only a few times. That's it. There was nothing magical about it. There was nothing between us. And there never will be."

"You know I love you, babe."

"Maybe you don't know what love is. Because I imagine that a man in love wouldn't beat the object of his affections to the point where she requires hospitalization."

"I did no such thing!" he exploded.

She was tired of going through the same ol', same ol' with this man. There had to be an end. "What do you want from me, Ned?" she asked again.

"You're never coming back to me, are you?" Ned asked, using his calm tone again. He spoke as if the realization had just dawned on him.

"There's nothing to come back to. You and I were never a couple. I hope you find a way to get that through your head."

"Does that mean you don't want to help your brother out of the jam he's gotten himself into?"

That wasn't fair. Of course, she wanted to help Solomon. Closing her eyes, she bit the bullet. "What do I have to do?"

"Just meet me for breakfast. That's all I'm asking. If you do that, then I'll tell the judge that I provoked your brother."

"And all I have to do is have breakfast with you?"

"Me and one of my business associates."

"I don't like where this is going, Ned."

"No funny business. I just want you to have breakfast with us. Your beauty is bound to distract him enough to let me close the deal while he's staring at you."

After what he'd done to her, he really wanted to use her like a little Barbie doll? The thought of doing anything to help Ned disgusted her. But she didn't want to be responsible for any additional drama in the life of her family. She'd caused them enough trouble by paying Summer Jones to make false accusations against her father, which had ended up unveiling the scandal that Summer's daughter, Winter, was the daughter of Leah's brother Adam.

Leah sighed, feeling helpless to do anything but what Ned was asking of her. "Where do you want to meet?" she asked him.

He gave her the name of the restaurant and the address. "Be there in half an hour, okay?"

"Fine," Leah said. "But I can't stay long, because I have to get to work on time."

As she headed for the restaurant, Leah could scarcely believe she had just agreed to meet with a man against whom she had filed a restraining order. Even though she had acquiesced out of a desire to help Solomon, she knew in her heart that he would not approve. She pulled into a gas station, parked her car, and sat there, gripping the steering wheel, remembering how Ned had held her on the ground until she agreed with him that she was dumb and worthless. Sweat beaded across her forehead at the thought of such a thing happening to her again.

Ned would be proven right about her being dumb if she allowed herself to get within fifty feet of him. She picked up her cell phone again, dialed the service provider, and asked them to change her number.

Fifteen minutes later, after all the necessary protocol was complete, she tossed the phone back in her purse and headed to work.

Leah turned on the radio in an effort to get the sound of Ned's voice out of her head. Her mother always turned on praise CDs to soothe herself. Needing something to ease her troubled mind, Leah scanned the stations until she found one that played inspirational music. Marvin Sapp was singing "Praise Him in Advance." What struck Leah was the line about confusing the enemy with one's praise. She wondered if that was possible. And would it work on Ned? Maybe if she tried it, he would think that she'd gone insane and would finally leave her alone.

She giggled at her silly musings. But as she pulled into the parking lot at work, all her laughter dried up. Cory was standing outside the building, talking with a police officer whose squad car was parked out front.

"What's going on?" she asked Cory as she approached.

He pointed to the police car. "Check the backseat."

Ned was sitting there.

Her hand flew to her mouth as she tried to figure out what had happened in the space of time between her hanging up from the call with Ned and her driving to work.

"I saw him sitting in his car when I came in this morning," Cory told her. "I figured he was up to no good, so I called the police. They found a gun in his glove compartment."

"He came here to…kill me?" Leah started gasping for air as she realized how close she'd come to meeting her end. But why had he invited her to breakfast if he'd been planning to kill her at her office?

"Don't worry about it, Leah," Cory told her. "Remember, I've got your back. Nothing is going to happen to you."

Cory reminded her so much of her brother Solomon. The brother that she hadn't wanted. But these days, he was coming in handy, as Adam was still healing from the fallout with his wife while he struggled to give his children at least some sense of stability in their crazy, chaotic existence.

Leah had seen firsthand how devastating the enemy's forces could be. And she wouldn't allow Cory to get hurt trying to defend her. Ned was too slick and would find a way to hurt Cory, just as he had done to Solomon.

When the police officer finally left to haul Ned off to jail, she turned to Cory. "I think it's best that I make this my last day."

Cory put an arm around her shoulders and led her inside, into the small conference room to the left of the front door. Then he pulled her close and wrapped his arms around her. When they stepped apart, Cory told her, "You looked like you needed a hug."

She hated that he was right…and that his hug had felt so good and so right, at a time in her life when everything else was so wrong. But she didn't trust her feelings or her intuition anymore. If Cory felt good and right, then he had to be all wrong for her.

She started shaking as confusion and self-disgust swept over her. How had she been so blind to Ned's nefarious ways from the start?

"Leah, calm down," Cory urged her. "Why don't we sit and talk about this?"

"I—I've got to go," she stammered. "I don't want anyone else to get hurt because of the drama in my life. Especially one of your employees. Or you."

Cory took her hands in his, walked her over to the nearest chair, and helped her to sit. "That's what I want to talk to you about. Dean told me that he invited you on the retreat this weekend."

"He did, but I don't think I contributed enough to be included." Leah hung her head. She was so tired of feeling inferior. So tired of being out of place.

"Dean never would have finished the program for Pro-Site Two if you hadn't pulled things together for him. The man may be a genius, but he can't find his way to the corner store without a GPS. Dean knows he owes the completion of this project to you. That's why he invited you."

"Are you sure?" Leah had a hard time accepting that she had actually added value to this project. Most of the time, it seemed she was causing trouble and messing things up for everyone else.

"I'm positive," Cory told her. "And anyway, you could use an escape. Why don't you take the day off, go home, and pack your bags? You can meet us at the airport tomorrow morning. I'll have Brandy handle your plane tickets and resort reservations."

"Okay, Cory," Leah finally acquiesced. "If you think I've made enough of a contribution, then I'd love to go to the Bahamas this weekend."

Leah left the office feeling that she had made the right decision. She needed to relax and forget about the ex-boyfriend who was out to kill her.

The biggest hurdle now would be to explain to her parents why she had left work early and was now packing for a weekend in the Bahamas.

"I don't believe it!" her father exploded when she told him about Ned. He popped out of his chair and started pacing the floor. "This is too much. Why was he even in at your job, anyway?"

"I guess he has some free time and decided to use it to harass me."

Leah's mother shook her head. "What's wrong with him? Why won't he just leave you alone?"

"He works for Satan—that's why, Mama."

"And you think running off to the Bahamas for the weekend is going to stop him?" her mother asked.

"Maybe I should stay down there." Leah turned to her father. "Remember when you took us to the Caribbean when we were teens, and we saw that lady who stood on the corner with a fruit basket on her head and charged people a fee for having their picture taken with her? Maybe I could earn a living doing something like that."

"That's crazy, Leah. Why would you want to do that?" her mother asked.

"I don't. But I don't want to stay here, wondering what Ned's next move will be, either."

"Or maybe I should just go and have a chat with this insane man," her father said. "Maybe he will see the light after talking with a man of the cloth."

"No, Daddy. I made the mistake of getting involved with Ned, and I will find a way to get out of this situation. But the last thing I want is for anything to happen to you because of my poor decisions."

"Something has to be done. I'm not just going to sit idly by and let that man kill my daughter." He then wagged his forefinger accusingly at his wife. "And while you were keeping Leah's secret from me, Ned could have killed her, and there would have been nothing I could do to stop it."

"That's not fair, David," her mother said. "I didn't want to keep anything from you. But when that animal hurt Leah, she was so worried that you might have another heart attack if you knew the full extent of what had happened, she begged me not to tell you all the details."

He let out a loud sigh. "I'm just so upset. First, our little girl is nearly killed, and now she's running off to the Bahamas. How are we supposed to keep her safe while she's away?"

"I'll be okay, Daddy," Leah assured him. "I'm glad they invited me. This trip will give me some much-needed time to rest my mind and get back to enjoying life rather than living in constant fear."

"I wish you were sixteen again," he told her. "Then I could forbid this trip and send you to your room."

"Oh, Daddy." Leah kissed him on the forehead. "Sometimes, I wish I was sixteen again, too. Then I could go back and change some of the things that I did during my teenage years. My adult years, as well."

"You were a perfect angel during your teenage years," her mother told her.

"Oh, there were plenty of things I could've handled better."

Specifically, Leah was thinking about how she'd spent her adolescence being filled with jealousy of Larissa. She'd come to live with them at the age of twelve, when her own parents were no longer able to take care of her. And Leah had done everything in her power to make her feel unwelcome, all because she hadn't wanted to share her parents.

"Well, if you're set on going to the Bahamas, then I think we need another girls' shopping trip for some new swimsuits and sundresses. Don't you?" her mother asked, breaking into her thoughts.

"Not another girls' shopping trip," her father groaned. "My wallet can't handle it."

10

"Mama, you didn't have to bring me to the South Park Mall," Leah protested as her mother pulled into the parking lot outside Nordstrom. "We could have gone to Stein Mart, T.J.Maxx, or even Ross. I'm not making enough money to shop here."

"Hush, child. This shopping trip is on your daddy's credit card." Her mother giggled. "He won't know what hit him until he sees the bill."

Leah was still amazed whenever her mother went out of her way to do something nice for her. Yes, they were a close family. But Alma Davison didn't play. And Leah was still coming to understand the boundless quality of her mother's forgiving nature.

"Does that mean you've got me covered, too?" Tamara asked from the backseat, where she was buckled in next to Larissa.

"Now, Tamara," Leah chided her. "With that rich husband you landed, you don't need Mama and Daddy buying you anything. But if you want to trade my life for yours, I'm sure Mama will buy you some sympathy presents."

Tamara turned to Larissa. "When she puts it like that, I guess I'll stop begging." She gave Leah a playful shove as they climbed out of the car.

"I'm telling!" Leah taunted her.

"Don't you two start," their mother said sternly. "We haven't even gotten inside the mall yet. What are you, fourteen again?"

"She started it," Tamara said, pointing at Leah. "Didn't she, Larissa?"

Larissa backed up and waved a hand. "I'm not getting involved," Larissa said, backing away with a wave of her hand. "I brought my own credit cards to do some damage with."

"Okay, okay," Tamara said. "I'll spend my own money."

"You're just too spoiled, Tamara. That's the only reason you might expect Mama to take you shopping, even while you and Jonathan are worth millions."

"Well, I am the baby of the family, and the baby always gets what she wants." Tamara grinned. "But y'all are right. This shopping trip is about you, Leah. I might even buy you something to wear down in the Bahamas. You never know—you might meet a handsome Bahamian man and come home with a ring on your finger."

"I highly doubt that." Leah didn't even want to think about being in a relationship. Not while she was still dealing with all the drama stemming from her dates with Ned. "I wouldn't want to ruin anyone else's life along with mine."

"Your life isn't ruined," Larissa said, putting an arm around Leah. "I mean, come on—you have a good job, you work with nice people, and, to top it off, you have the most handsome godson in all the world."

"You're right about that. My little godson is so cute, I can barely stand it. The last time I was with him, he made me turn on a Fresh Beat Band CD so he could dance. He cracks me up."

"See? Your life doesn't feel so terrible when you're with baby Eric, now, does it?" her mother asked.

Leah nodded. "He brightens my days, for sure."

"Hey, Leah—what do you think of this number?" Tamara asked, holding up a red sleeveless floor-length dress that appeared to be quite formfitting. "Cory won't be able to resist you if you show up for dinner wearing this."

"If Cory and I have dinner together, it will be with the rest of the crew from the company. So, I doubt that what I wear will matter all that much. And anyway," Leah added, pointing at the beautiful gown, "that 'number' is fit for a movie actress on the red carpet or a model on the catwalk. Not for a lowly assistant like me."

"That's it," Larissa declared, stamping her foot. "If you put yourself down again, I'm going to make you wash out your mouth with soap. We weren't raised to think so little of ourselves. You remember that, okay?"

It did seem that she had nothing but negative things to say, of late. Leah would try to rein in her words from now on. "I'm sorry for my attitude," she apologized. "You all gave up time you could have spent with your husbands in order to hang out with me, and I've been nothing but miserable."

"We understand, honey," her mother told her.

"No, Mama. I'm not being fair to you all." She took the red dress from Tamara. "I'm going to try this on. But when I come back out, I don't want to talk about me with a Bahamian man or with Cory. I just want to hear about you and your wonderful husbands. It brings me joy to know that my girls are happy and that they made the right decisions where men are concerned."

As Leah stepped into the dressing room, she could hear the other three whispering together.

"I feel so bad for Leah, Mama," Tamara said in a hushed tone. "I don't know what to do."

"It breaks my heart to think of what happened to her," Larissa put in. "She and Adam are both having such a tough time of it right now. I want to do something to help them."

"Don't worry about Adam," Leah's mother said. "I've got something in mind for him. As for Leah, we just have to do what she has asked us to, and give her some space."

Leah stepped out of the dressing room feeling like a fashion model, and the others told her she looked like one. Blushing, she said, "I guess red's a good color for me, huh?"

"I think this one's a keeper," Tamara said.

Leah twirled around, watching her reflection in the mirror. "It sure is."

After her mother had paid for the dress, the women moved on to Neiman Marcus. As they shopped, Leah continued asking her mother and her sisters about their marriages. All three of them had found true love—something Leah desperately needed to believe in again.

That night, after a successful day of shopping, the entire family gathered at Leah's parents' house for dinner. Her mother had prepared pork roast with cabbage and au gratin potatoes—Adam's favorite. He surveyed the dishes on the table, then said, "Don't tell me—there's a red velvet cake in the kitchen."

"Of course," their mother said, beaming.

"Is it my birthday, and I just forgot or something?" he asked with a grin.

"I delight in making my son happy. Is there something wrong with that?" she asked.

The family hadn't seen very many smiles from Adam since his ex-wife had tried to kill him before it was discovered that she had a mental illness.

As everyone took a seat, Leah noticed that there was an extra chair next to Adam. She sent her mother a questioning glance, but her mother just frowned and shook her head.

Whatever, Leah thought. She figured her mother had the right to do whatever she wanted to do for Adam.

"Let's go before the Lord and thank Him for all this wonderful food," her father said.

Leah looked around the table as all the heads bowed and eyes closed. She kept her eyes open, still not in a praying mood.

Her father began, "Gracious God, we thank You for the food we are about to receive. We ask that it would nourish our bodies, and we claim that if there be any impurities in our food, that You cast them out, because they are not worthy of Your children. And, Father, as a special request, I ask that You would go with my daughter Leah as she journeys with her coworkers to the Bahamas. I wish that I could be with my children at all times to watch over them and keep them safe; but I am thankful that You have promised to do so in my stead. So, I'm asking that You would send Your mighty warrior angels to encamp around her and bring her back home to us safe and sound."

"In Jesus' name we pray, amen," Leah's mother finished for him, then jumped up when the doorbell rang. "I'll get it."

She rushed out of the room as if she were going to admit Jesus Himself to their gathering and didn't want to keep Him waiting even one second longer than necessary.

She returned moments later, followed by none other than Chef Marla Williams. "Everybody, meet Marla Williams. She's the one who prepared that wonderful dinner we enjoyed a few weeks ago." Then she made the introductions.

"Sorry I'm late," Marla told the group. "Traffic was backed up along the interstate due to a big accident."

"You're right on time," Leah's father assured her. "We just sat down."

Marla set a basket on the table. "I baked some dinner rolls."

Leah's mother gave her a hug. "Bless you. We will really appreciate these, as I didn't get a chance to make any myself." Then she gestured to the empty chair. "Marla, why don't you sit down right there next to Adam?"

"And start passing that bread around," Leah's father said. "If that meal you made us at the Merrimont was any indication, these are bound to be the best dinner rolls we've ever tasted. From the kitchen of a professional chef."

"Hardly professional," Marla said shyly. "I'm still in cooking school, and even so, cooking's just a hobby. My true passion is music."

"Is it, now?" Adam asked, sounding intrigued. "How do you have time to do both?"

"I'm a music teacher by profession, so I have the summers off, and I've spent the last two taking classes at the culinary institute."

"A music teacher, huh?" Leah's father asked, then glanced at his wife before asking, "Do you play the piano?"

"Oh, yes," Marla said with a nod. "In fact, I served as the minister of music at my former church. But I haven't played in church since moving here for my teaching assignment."

Leah knew just what her mother was up to, and she couldn't help it—she burst out laughing.

Everyone turned to her, eyeing her as if she were crazy.

She tried to assure them that it was nothing, but her laughter kept her from speaking coherently. The giggles made her feel good, like balm to her soul.

"Leah, why don't you help me in the kitchen?" her mother said, then helped Leah out of her seat and out of the dining room.

"Was it something I said?" Leah heard Marla ask her family.

"Not at all," her father assured their guest. "Leah hasn't laughed in a very long time, but I'm sure she wasn't laughing at you."

In the kitchen, Leah finally regained her composure. "I'm sorry, Mama. I really am."

"What's wrong with you?" Her mother gave her a gentle swat on the arm. "We don't treat guests like that in this house. Why did you have to embarrass Marla like that?"

"I didn't mean to embarrass Marla, but I needed that laugh. Thank you, Mama." She hugged her mother and kissed her on the cheek. "Because of your scheming, I feel so much better."

"Scheming?" Her mother planted her hands on her hips. "I don't know what you're talking about, Leah Davison. I'm not scheming up anything."

"Oh, really?" Leah folded her arms across her chest and narrowed her eyes. "Are you going to tell me that little miss Betty Crocker out there isn't here because you think she would be perfect for the minister of music position that just became available at the church…and perfect for your son who needs a wife?"

Her mother waved her off, but Leah knew she was right. "You have a very active imagination, Leah. Just stop that laughing and help me deliver the salad plates."

The moment they reentered the dining room, Leah's father said, "Alma, good news! Marla has agreed to interview for the position of minister of music at the church."

"That's wonderful, David." Her mother smiled with feigned surprise. "I think Marla would be an excellent addition to our church staff."

Leah had to call on the powers of the Holy Ghost, the angels, and Jesus Himself to keep from bursting out laughing again. By some miracle, she managed to take her seat and shovel enough food in her mouth so that she would remain silent. But she was happy for Adam. Because, if her mother was right about this girl, Adam's heart would soon be leaping again.

Leah would be leaving for the Bahamas in the morning, meaning she wouldn't be around as her mother's scheme unfolded. Not wanting to miss out, she said, "Why don't you let Marla use the piano in the living room for an audition?"

"Marla might not be prepared right at this minute, Leah," her mother said, giving her the look that said, *Stop it right now.* "Give her a few days to pull something together."

"Oh, I'm up for the challenge," Marla said with a smile. "I would love to play for you all."

"Why don't we take our dessert in the living room?" Leah's father suggested. "It'll be like a private concert."

"I think that's an excellent idea," Leah said, winking at her mother.

When the meal was over and the cake had been cut, they carried their plates into the living room, where Marla sat down at the piano and astounded them with her beautiful playing. But that was only half the story. She opened her mouth and began to sing, first a song by Marvin Sapp and then one by Yolanda Adams. And she did both songs better than the original versions.

Leah looked at Adam. He appeared completely captivated.

Then she smiled at her mother, whose intuition never ceased to amaze her. Marla would be the perfect fit for the church. Would she also be the one to help heal Adam's wounded heart?

11

Leah hadn't wreaked havoc only in her father's life after discovering that he had a son with another woman; she had destroyed Adam's life, as well. Once it had come to light that the woman Leah had hired to extort money from her father was actually the mother of Adam's illegitimate child, Winter, things had gone from bad to worse. Because Adam's wife had completely lost her mind.

And Leah blamed herself for the demise of Adam's marriage. Her mind drifted back a few years to the last time that Adam had been in intensive care. Leah had blamed herself for that incident, as well....

Adam had been shot and was now in surgery. Everybody was feeling pretty low, but Leah felt the worst. She was hunched in a chair against the wall in a nearby alcove, her head down, her arms wrapped around herself, like a child who'd been ordered to the corner for a time-out.

Solomon scooted a chair over and sat next to her. When she looked up at him with questioning eyes, he said, "I thought you might want some company."

Leah scoffed. "Are you sure you want to do that? Being in company with me might get you exiled from this family."

Solomon chuckled. "I've already been exiled for most of my life, remember? I'm the half brother you knew nothing about until this year."

"Maybe you're right," Leah said with a sigh. "What else can they do to you besides take you out of the will? The truth is, Adam and I would love it if they did that." She was on the verge of sobbing as she added, "But who knows if Adam will outlive our parents? Maybe it will be his name that's taken out of the will."

"Don't do this to yourself, Leah," Solomon pleaded. "You've got to have faith. I believe that God is able to do the impossible. What about you?"

She shook her head. "I used to believe. Then again, I used to believe in Santa Claus and the Easter bunny, too. Shows how much I know."

"Adam needs you to be strong for him," Solomon told her. "He's in there fighting for his life, and he needs us to be praying and believing that God can bring him out of the nightmare he's in. Do you think you'd be willing to pray along with me, Larissa, and Tamara?"

Chewing her lip and twirling her hair around her finger, Leah said, "They don't want me messing up their prayers."

"I don't think you'd be 'messing up' anything. And I think Larissa and Tamara need just as much support as you do right now. I can see how much you're hurting, and I know that you love your brother and wouldn't have wanted anything like this to happen to him."

She unfolded her arms and turned toward Solomon. "Why are you being so nice to me? I sure haven't been nice to you."

"We're family, right?"

Leah nodded without hesitation this time.

Solomon grabbed hold of her hand, helped her stand up, and led her over to Larissa and Tamara. "Do you two mind if we join you?" he asked them.

Tamara moved over and patted the seat next to her. "Take a load off."

"That's just what we need to do," Solomon said. "Would you two join hands with us as we pray for a speedy recovery for Adam? I think Leah would feel a lot better if we did that."

Larissa popped up from her chair. "Absolutely. I'd love to."

Tamara was a little slower to stand, but she soon clasped hands with Leah and Solomon. "We did a group prayer earlier with Mama and Daddy, but I guess I don't see the harm in praying again."

After they had prayed, tears were streaming down Leah's face. Larissa reached over with a tissue and wiped her cheeks. "We've done enough crying for today," she said. "Adam is going to be all right. Let's just keep praying for him."

Solomon had been there for Leah during her time of need, but Tamara was the one comforting her now. "Stop crying, Leah. This is not your fault. If Portia harmed Adam, then she is to blame."

"But Portia never would have been so jealous if I hadn't brought Summer and Winter back into Adam's life in the first place."

Leah closed her eyes for a silent prayer that her family wouldn't continue to pay for this thing that she had set in motion after finding out about their father's secret son. It was time for their family to heal, once and for all.

Marla finished playing the piano and then stood to a round of applause. She gave a tiny bow. "Thank you. I'm so glad you enjoyed it."

Soon, she was talking business with Leah's parents. Tamara, Jonathan, Solomon, and Larissa headed back to the dining room to start cleaning up. That's when Leah turned to Adam. "We haven't seen much of you lately," she told him. "How have you been doing?"

Adam shrugged. "To tell you the truth, it's really been hard. My children miss their mother, and even though the divorce is final, I keep wondering if I made a mistake by not sticking by her."

Putting a hand on Adam's shoulder, she told him, "You did stick by her. Even after you were shot by that horrible cousin of hers, you stayed in that house and tried to make your marriage work. How much more were you supposed to take?"

"I don't know," Adam answered honestly. "But maybe I shouldn't have snuck around to see Winter without telling Portia what I was doing."

"Winter is your daughter, Adam. You have a right to see her. It's like what Mama did to Daddy with Solomon all over again. And you saw how angry Solomon was with this entire family because he had been shut out. Do you really want Winter to grow up thinking that you don't care enough to be in her life?" Leah couldn't believe she had once believed that her family was perfect and pious. The truth was, they were just as flawed as the next family.

"So then, I ended up sneaking around to see my daughter, just like Daddy snuck around taking pictures of Solomon, just so he could share some part of Solomon's life." He shook his head. "I just don't see how two wrongs make a right."

"Adam, Portia ran you over with her car. You don't owe that woman anything else."

Leah didn't understand why her brother was placing all the blame on himself. He'd been married to a horrible woman who'd done horrible things to him. Adam was a very spiritual man, so Leah understood why he had a problem with divorce. But Leah still remembered the trauma her family had gone through at the hospital when they didn't know whether Adam was going to live or die....

Leah was curled up in the same alcove she'd sat the last time Adam had been in intensive care. Solomon was talking with Larissa, so

Tamara crossed the room and stood beside her sister. "Hey, big sis. You got room for one more over here on the pity party side of the room?"

"What's your pity party about?" Leah asked without looking up.

"Let's see…." Tamara sat down next to her sister. "My sister-in-law tried to murder my brother. My sister blames herself. And—oh, yeah. I got fired today."

Leah sat up and spun around in her seat. "You were fired for coming home to check on Adam?"

Tamara shook her head. "I think it had more to do with my having a rocky start on the job and then having the nerve to leave town without advance notice."

"Well, it's their loss."

"Not too much of a loss, but I appreciate your saying that, Sis." Tamara leaned over and pulled Leah into an embrace. "Now, what about you?"

Leah wiped the tears from her eyes. "What about me?"

"When are you going to realize that God has forgiven you for what you tried to do to Daddy? Our entire family has forgiven you. When will you let go of the guilt you've put on yourself?"

"It sounds so simple when you say it."

"I realize it can be hard to believe it for yourself," Tamara said. "It's like how I understood the concept of forgiveness for everybody except my own father. I tried to punish Daddy by moving as far away as I could. But I ended up missing you all so much that the only person I really punished was myself."

"We missed you, too. And I'll take what you just said to heart."

"Please do, because Adam isn't back there fighting for his life because of anything you did." Tamara pointed toward the double doors of the intensive care unit. "He's back there because of the woman the police arrested."

"Why didn't he divorce that woman?" Leah asked….

Well, Adam finally had divorced Portia, and now it was time for him to begin living again. And if her brother got his life back, it would finally free Leah from at least some of the guilt she felt for causing so much damage to her family. That would be the day that Leah would be able to go on with her life.

"I'm sorry for messing things up for you, Adam," she told him. "If I could do anything to make it better, I'd do it in a minute."

"I know," he said, nodding.

"Time heals all wounds, right?"

"Let's hope so."

Leah was hoping that her statement was true not only for Adam but also for herself. Because her wounds still hadn't healed, either. Maybe this trip to the Bahamas would be the healing balm that she needed at this point in her life.

12

The Atlantis Resort was a sight to behold. There was something spectacular to see everywhere Leah turned. From the pools to the water slides, the river rides to the movie theaters, on and on it went. The place was far too luxurious for the wallet of a lowly assistant like her—especially the Royal Towers, where they were staying.

Dean had told her that she would be sharing a room with Brandy, but when she checked in at the registration desk, Leah was pleasantly surprised to discover that they would, in fact, have their own rooms. Granted, these rooms were much smaller than the suites the executives occupied, but Leah didn't care. She was on Paradise Island in the

Bahamas, over seven hundred miles away from Ned, and she was going to enjoy every minute of her time.

She sat down on her bed, took out her cell phone, and called home, as promised, to let her parents know that she'd made it there without incident. The phone rang a few times before her mother picked up.

"How was the flight?" her mother wanted to know.

"Really smooth," Leah said. "Probably one of the calmest flights I've ever been on."

"That just shows that God answers prayers," her mother told her.

Leah thought that the pilots deserved a bit of credit, but she wouldn't say that to her mother. "I'm in my room now. I just wanted to let you know that I made it safely."

"I'm so glad you called. I'll let everyone else know." Her mother paused for a moment. "Try to enjoy yourself, sweetie."

"I will, Mama."

When they'd said their good-byes, Leah put the phone down and walked over to the floor-to-ceiling windows in her room. She opened the curtains wide and looked down at the clear blue water before her. The sight was incredibly calming, and Leah felt completely at peace. She knew now that she'd made the right decision in coming on the trip.

A knock on her door broke her trancelike stare at the ocean. "Who is it?"

"It's me, girl. Brandy."

Leah went to the door and checked the peephole, just to make sure. There stood her coworker, dressed in a bathing suit with a towel wrapped around her waist.

She opened the door with a smile.

"A few of us are heading to the pool," Brandy told her. "Do you want to come along?"

"Sounds good," Leah said. "Do you mind waiting while I change?"

"Not at all."

She let Brandy into the room, then ducked inside the massive bathroom to put on her aqua swimsuit. When she emerged, she grabbed her beach bag, which she'd already filled with a water bottle, the novel she'd brought to read, a beach towel, a small bottle of sunblock, and a sun visor. Then she rummaged around in her purse for a few other items to add. As she grabbed her mints, Leah caught sight of the pepper spray she'd purchased to protect herself from Ned. She grabbed hold of it, getting ready to put it in her beach bag. But then she had a strange feeling, almost like someone whispering in her ear, telling her to put the pepper spray in the drawer of the nightstand next to her bed. Figuring there was no way Ned had followed her here, she heeded the inclination and left it there before following Brandy from the room.

Down at the pool, Leah tried to concentrate on her book, but Cory was distracting her something fierce. She'd never imagined that he would look so good in swim trunks, but his biceps, triceps, and washboard abs were doing a number on her. She wanted to call her mother and ask for prayer for to get the demon of lust off her back. She had been celibate since she was old enough to make that decision, and she intended to stay that way until she'd walked down the aisle and said "I do" to the man to whom she would pledge her fidelity for life.

"Come on, Leah." Cory splashed water on her. "Put that book down and have some fun."

She didn't want to be anywhere near Cory, so she pointed at Dean, stretched out on a lounge chair with a stack of documents in front of him. "He's reading, too."

"Yeah, but Dean has always been a party pooper. You don't want to end up like him." Cory got out of the pool and sauntered toward her.

Water dripped off his body like summer rain on a sun-scorched beach. Leah was wishing for a drought. She jumped off the lounge chair and tucked her book in her beach bag. "I've got to go back to my room."

"What's wrong with you?" Cory asked as she rushed past him.

"I'll be back."

She had to get away from Cory. Judging from her track record, any man to whom she was attracted ended up having a huge character flaw. As far as Leah was concerned, if she liked Cory, there was probably something wrong with him. So, she was going to stay as far away from him as possible. She had escaped from Ned, and now she needed to escape from Cory. Needed to run away from false love that sought only to bring her harm. From this day forward, she wanted nothing to do with it.

Cory caught up with her at the elevators. "Did I do something to upset you?" he asked, drying himself off with the towel he'd grabbed.

She shook her head. "No, it's not you. It's just…I need to get away."

Smiling that gorgeous grin of his, Cory said, "That's what this trip is all about."

"What I'm trying to say is, I…I want to explore the island."

"Okay, then I'll go with you."

"No," she practically shouted in his face.

"I can't let you go off on your own, Leah. Your father would never forgive me if you turned up missing. We are not in North Carolina. You don't know this place like the back of your hand, so I think it's best if we stick together."

She wanted to argue, but, deep down, she knew he was right. It would be foolish to go off exploring alone. "Okay," she agreed, "but put some clothes on first."

Cory laughed. "I guess I shouldn't punish the Bahamian women with this view. I'll go get changed and meet you back here in twenty minutes, okay?"

When Cory got off the elevator on his floor, Leah couldn't help but sneak another glance. She couldn't think of a single woman who wouldn't consider his athletic physique something lovely to behold indeed. She fanned herself as she channeled her mother. "I need to get my mind on Jesus."

When they met up in the lobby, Leah was wearing a sundress she'd bought the day before. Cory had on a pair of tan shorts with a polo shirt. He grabbed her hand. "Come on," he said. "I know just the place to explore."

They hopped in his rental car and left the resort. Their first stop was Bay Street for some duty-free shopping. But as Leah looked around at the shops carrying high-end jewelry, clothing, and other merchandise, she told him, "Tax free or not, I can't afford this place."

"At least look at some of this stuff before you judge."

Cory ducked inside a jewelry store and asked to see a tennis bracelet. As the jeweler fastened the white gold bracelet with sparkling diamonds to her arm, Leah was captivated by its beauty. But when she wondered what it would cost her to accept such a gift, suddenly, the bracelet wasn't so beautiful anymore. She took it off and handed it back to the jeweler. "I'm ready to go," she told Cory.

"What's your hurry?" he asked, searching her face. "Don't you like the bracelet?"

"Of course, I like the bracelet. But it's three thousand dollars. I don't have that kind of money."

"What if I wanted to buy it for you?" Cory asked. His eyes locked on hers, sending her messages she wasn't prepared to receive.

Leah folded her arms across her chest. "It's still too expensive for me."

Blinking, he stepped back a bit. "What's that supposed to mean?"

"It means I'm not going to sleep with you just because you buy me a diamond bracelet."

"Whoa." Cory lifted his hands in surrender. "I know that Ned deeply hurt you. And maybe a few other men have done unseemly things to you, as well. But that doesn't give you the right to assume that I'm just like them." Then he stormed out of the jewelry shop.

Leah gave the jeweler an apologetic half smile before exiting the store, hoping that Cory hadn't been angry enough to leave her to find her way back to the Atlantis on her own. But when she turned the corner and saw the rental car, she breathed easer. Cory was a gentleman, just as he'd been back in high school, always opening doors for the ladies and never disparaging even the cruelest of ex-girlfriends. His jerk of a best friend had been the total opposite and had treated Leah horribly.

When she reached the car, Cory leaned across the console and opened the passenger door from the inside.

"Thanks," she said as she got in.

He didn't respond but just started the car and drove.

"Where are we?" Leah asked as he parked again a few minutes later.

"The Straw Market. A place where you can shop without needing to sell your body for the privilege."

She knew that she owed Cory an apology, but her pride wouldn't let her offer one right now. She opened the door, got out of the car, and started exploring the vendors' wares. If Cory wanted to hold a grudge, that was on him. She hadn't asked him to tag along, so he could either change his attitude or go on back to the hotel.

Leah spotted some cute little T-shirts that read "Bahama Mama" that had Tamara and Larissa's names all over them. When she saw the sign advertising three for ten dollars, she grabbed another one for her mother. In the back of the store, a Gucci wallet caught her eye. It was selling for twenty bucks, so Leah knew that it was a knockoff, but she picked it up anyway.

Cory stepped outside of the store to take a business call. When he came back inside, he had a perplexed expression on his face. Leah wanted to take his mind off whatever was bothering him, so she picked up a straw hat with the word "Bahamas" stitched across the front and set it on his head. "I knew it would look awesome on you," she said.

Cory checked his reflection in the wall mirror nearby, then tilted the hat with a grin. "I think you're right. I like it."

"Take it off. I'll buy it for you."

"Oh, no." Cory shook a finger at her. "I'm not about to trade myself for a twelve-dollar straw hat."

Feeling remorseful over her mean-spirited comment, she twisted her lip, then said, "I'm sorry, Cory. I shouldn't have said those things to you in the jewelry store."

He took off the hat and twirled it in his hands. "But you did say them. And I'd like to know why."

She sighed. "I was wrong. Let's just leave it at that, okay?" She turned away from him and carried her T-shirts to the checkout counter.

After she'd traded three tens for a touristy-looking bag containing the T-shirts, Cory grabbed her arm and ushered her out of the store. "I don't want to leave it at that," he told her. "I'd like to know how someone as beautiful and vivacious as you could have fallen so low to assume that a man who wanted to buy you something pretty did so with ulterior motives."

"I don't want to do this, Cory," she said, shaking her head. "I said I'm sorry. Please let it go."

"What if I don't want to let it go?"

They were standing so close that she could feel the heat rising off him as his nostrils flared. But he didn't have a right to be angry with her.

She snatched her arm free from him. "Then go back to the hotel and leave me alone."

13

Cory had better things to do than chase a woman who didn't want to be caught. He had never been spoken to the way Leah had spoken to him. Most of the women he had dated appreciated the gifts he gave them. Then again, he wasn't dating Leah; obviously, he never would. He simply needed to get those silly high school dreams out of his head. He was a grown man now, and if a troubled woman wanted nothing to do with him, he would take the hint and move on.

They were having dinner beneath the stars at the Ocean Club—one of the premier dining spots on Paradise Island. Cory dressed in his Dolce & Gabbana white linen blazer and a pair of black slacks. The ensemble was stylish without being too formal.

Amid the elegant décor and romantic ambiance, Cory was all business as he shook hands and networked. He had things on his mind that couldn't be discussed during a night of celebration.

Then Leah walked in and knocked him off his game with that dress she was wearing. Cory silently fumed as all the other men present fell over themselves in their rush to get an audience with her. He doubted he'd be able to watch Leah prance around with a long cast of admirers all night, so he clasped his hands and cleared his throat to get everyone's attention, then suggested they sit down and order dinner.

Several members of the group shot questioning glances his way. One actually accused him of being the fun police, but he didn't care. Cory didn't owe any of them an explanation. As far as he was concerned, they could just sit down, shut up, eat, and leave him alone. He was the leader of the bunch, so he couldn't just go to the back of the room and ignore everyone, even though that was just what he wanted to do.

"Hey, buddy. You want to tone it down? I'm getting questions about your mood," Dean told him as they sat down together at one of the round tables near to the candlelit fountain pool.

"Who said what about my mood?" Cory asked, feeling ready and willing to fire the culprit.

Dean leaned closer and whispered, "If you want her so bad, why don't you just tell her to come to your room tonight?"

The suggestion disgusted him. "I don't know what you're talking about." Cory had never discussed his love life with Dean, and he wasn't about to start tonight. Especially since the love going on between him and Leah was completely one-sided.

Dean looked over his shoulder, then turned back to Cory. "All I'm saying is, Larry looks like he's about to make a move. So, if you're interested, you'd better stop acting like a choirboy and get at her."

Cory turned to his business partner and blurted out, "She's not interested in me, okay? So just leave it alone." Then he closed his eyes, trying to block out the pain the admission had caused him. Why had

God allowed him to spend so many years dreaming about a woman who was off-limits? And why had he been fool enough to convince her to take this trip?

"I'm sorry," Dean said. "I didn't mean to make assumptions."

"Don't worry about it." Cory started in on his dinner. He smiled and spoke at the appropriate times, but as soon as the meal was over, he excused himself and went for a walk on the beach.

He needed to put as much distance between him and Leah as possible. After having time to think about it, Cory understood that offering to purchase a bracelet worth three grand for a woman he wasn't even dating was too extravagant. So, he wasn't upset about the refusal of the bracelet. It was the way she'd refused it that was sticking in his gut. She'd treated him as if he were some slimy guy who preyed on every woman who stepped off the bus in a new city. Like he was going to wine and dine her, then put her on the stroll.

Leah wasn't the same girl he'd pined over since high school. With a heavy heart, Cory accepted that fact. He also accepted the fact that it was time to stop dreaming and to start moving forward with his life. He picked up a rock and tossed it into the ocean waves. Tiffany had been after him to make a commitment, either way. She was tired of wondering whether they were in a relationship. Cory had been prepared to tell her that they weren't, but maybe Tiffany was right for him, after all. He threw another rock, then lifted his head heavenward, praying for an answer. But Cory also knew that he wouldn't be able to do anything about his love life until his business affairs were squared away. And with the news he'd just received from his financial consultant, that wouldn't happen anytime soon.

His mother had raised him to trust in God. When he was little, she would run through the house shouting praises to a God that Cory couldn't see or touch. He hadn't understood it back then, but every time something good happened for their family—his dad got a promotion, Cory made the basketball team, they moved into a bigger house—his mother would tell him, "I prayed for that. Now I need to go thank and praise the Lord for bringing it to pass."

Right now, Cory was praying for the Lord to do something for him. He'd been highly successful and made tons of money. But Cory still felt as if he was in wait mode. "Can You please make it plain to me, Lord? Help me figure out what's going on with my life."

⟆

Alma Davison didn't know why she couldn't sleep. But an uneasy feeling had seized her and refused to let go.

She rolled over in bed and nudged her husband. "David? You asleep?"

David only grunted.

Alma nudged him again. "Wake up."

"Huh? What's wrong?"

"I don't know," Alma told him. "But I feel like we need to pray."

"Then let's get to it." David sat up in bed and took Alma's hands in his. Then he began to pray as if lightning would strike them if they didn't call on God to move the tide of the storm. Since they didn't know which one of their children was in trouble, the Davisons started praying in tongues, believing that God was well able to translate this message from the Holy Spirit and to fight their battle for them.

⟆

The Lord God Almighty was seated on His throne. The twenty-four elders surrounded Him, also seated on thrones, and clothed in radiant white robes. They wore crowns of gold on their heads.

Seven lamps of fire were burning, and a sea of crystal lay at the Master's feet. In the midst of the throne and all around it were four living creatures with eyes covering their entire bodies. The first living creature was like a lion, the second a calf, the third a man, and the fourth a flying eagle. Each of the creatures had six wings. Day and night, they moved without ceasing, soaring high above the thrones on their massive wings. Generating cool winds throughout heaven, they bellowed continuously to their King, crying, "Holy, holy, holy, Lord God Almighty, who was, and is, and is to come!"

The twenty-four elders fell down before Him and worshipped, saying, "You are worthy, O Lord, to receive glory and honor and power; for You created all things, and by Your will they exist and were created." They threw their crowns before the throne in adoration.

Then thunder rolled and lightning sparkled from the throne of grace. Michael's glorious nine-foot form stood. His colorful wings glistened as they flapped in the air. "Yes, my Lord," he said, accepting the scrolls from the Omnipotent hand that held them.

Taking his marching orders, Michael left the throne room to confer with Aaron, the captain of the host of warrior angels. As he walked through the heavens, Michael couldn't help but take in the beauty of it all. There were unnumbered mansions in the inner court, with room enough for everyone. But the beauty and splendor of heaven would be enjoyed only by the few who served God. As he passed by the room of tears, he glanced inside and shook his head in wonderment. It still amazed him that God would find the tears of humans so precious that He would bottle and preserve them in such a gloriously bright, white space.

The tree of life stood, bold and beautiful, in the middle of the outer court. Its leaves were a heavenly green, and its fruit was succulent and enjoyed by all. Sweet, blissful music could be heard throughout the great expanse of heaven. It was the harp, but it was better than any harp on earth; it was the guitar, but it was better than any guitar on earth.

There were thousands upon thousands of saints moving through the joys of heaven, clothed in glistening white robes, and with bare feet. Many had crowns on their heads with various types of jewels embedded in them—jewels representing the individuals they had helped lead to Christ while on earth.

On the opposite side of the outer court stood a great multitude of warrior angels. Their appearance was that of beauty and majesty. They wore white radiant garments embellished with gold-edged trim. At the waist, each of them wore a huge golden sword, and they had large white wings flapping from behind. The outer court was like a waiting room. The saints were waiting to be admitted into the inner court and, some, to the Holy of Holies.

The warrior angels awaited their next assignments. Right now, a great commotion was going on among the angels. They were anxious, for something big was about to happen—they just knew it. Some asked if Michael would greet them today. To this day, the angels in heaven remained in awe of the one angel who was able to meet Lucifer in battle and come out victorious every time. Even Gabriel had needed Michael's help when Lucifer had attacked him. They all admired their general and longed for a glimpse of him.

Captain Aaron lifted his hand, silencing the angels. "Brothers, calm yourselves. Evil is running rampant on the earth, so our general is very busy putting out many fires. We do not know when he will call upon this host again, but we will be ready when he does."

The angels lifted their swords and shouted, "We will be ready." Their job was to fight and to destroy the works of the enemy, as God gave them leave to do so. This host of angels had won many battles and had aided numerous humans in bringing souls to the Lord. They were humbly elite—they got the job done.

For this reason, Michael met with their captain and provided as many assignments as he could to their group. He was back today with a family they were familiar with. Michael smiled as he approached the group. "Did my ears hear the sound of angels ready to do battle?"

The host of angels nearly burst with excitement as their general presented himself before them.

Captain Aaron quieted them once again. "Let's hear what the general has to say."

Michael stood in front of Aaron. His sword was longer and heavier than that of the captain of the host. Jewels were embedded throughout the handle of this massive sword, a symbol of his many victories. The belt where his sword was holstered sparkled with the gold of heaven. Michael had defeated the Prince of Persia more times than he cared to remember. But the enemy was getting stronger as his time drew near.

Michael eagerly awaited their next meeting. It would be their last. "The prayers of the Davison family have risen to heaven once more," he said. "I realize that you lost a great number of warriors in our last battle with the wicked one, and this battle will be no easier. I must know if your troops are prepared for a new battle of great magnitude."

"We are always ready, General," Captain Aaron replied. "You give the command, and we will fight until there is no more fight left in us."

"Good," Michael said, then handed him the assignment.

Captain Aaron nodded. "Consider it handled."

14

While Cory stood on the beach, contemplating the very real possibility that he would lose in business and in love in the same weekend, an angel stood between heaven and earth, beckoning Cory to follow him.

The waters of the ocean shimmered with otherworldly beauty as the array of colors blended and stretched out, as if a path to someplace wondrous was being set before his eyes. Cory was compelled to walk the beach, following the brilliant colors. "Where you lead, I will follow," he said out loud, trusting that God was listening.

"Come on, Leah. Let's take a walk on the beach," said Larry, one of the IT guys, as he took off his shoes and rolled up his pant legs.

"You go ahead," she told him, shaking her head. "I'm just going to sit here for a while."

"Suit yourself." Larry turned to Brandy. "Walk with me?"

Brandy took off her heels and followed Larry and a few others down the beach.

Leah had seen Cory leave the party and head down to the beach almost half an hour earlier. He'd appeared to be in a foul mood, and Leah had a feeling that she was responsible for it. But she had already apologized, so she didn't understand why he couldn't just accept her apology and be cool about it.

Cory had been good to her. He'd given her a job and had taken steps to protect her from Ned. And what had she done but offend him? That had not been her intent. She just didn't know how to relate to men anymore.

"Penny for your thoughts," Dean said as he sat down next to her, drinks in both hands. He held one out to her.

Leah stared at the glass, remembering the time right after college when the guy she was dating had tried to slip something in her drink. From that point on, Leah had made it a practice never to accept a cup if she hadn't witnessed its being filled with the contents. "No, thank you. I just drank a tall glass of lemonade."

Grinning, Dean said, "More for me."

She smiled back. "You seem a lot more relaxed this weekend," she told him. "I'm glad the demo of the new site went over well."

"It did," Dean said, leaning back and taking a sip of his drink. "Now Cory's trying to figure out a way around another problem so we can get the IPO to go through."

"What's wrong? Why would Cory have a problem with the initial public offering if the new site is doing well?"

Dean took another swig of his drink, then looked into her eyes. "You're beautiful, you know that?"

Most of the time, when someone used the word "beautiful" to describe one of the Davison sisters, he was referring to Tamara or Larissa. Oh, Leah knew that she was pretty; but next to them, she just never seemed to measure up in the looks department. So, for Dean to be spouting off about how beautiful she was, Leah figured he'd probably had too much to drink. She wanted to create some space between herself and her boss before he started in on that second glass, so she stood.

"Leaving so soon?"

She nodded. "I think I'll turn in for the night. I have a book I want to finish."

"You're going to miss all the fun."

"I've had plenty of fun already," she said with a smile, then headed back to her hotel room.

⌒

Alma couldn't stop tossing and turning in bed.

"Still can't sleep?" David asked groggily.

She sat up, turned on the light, and grabbed his hand. "I'm worried, David. I think Leah's in trouble."

Her husband rubbed his eyes with his free hand. "Leah is far away from Ned. I'm sure she's fine. I was thinking that your concerns had more to do with Adam. He's been so down in the dumps lately that I really worry about him."

Alma shook her head. "It's Leah. I'm sure of it. Something has happened, David. I don't know what, but she's in trouble. We need to pray again."

David jumped out of bed and reached for the telephone. "Let's call her and see what's going on."

"Let's pray first. Then you can call."

David vacillated for a few seconds before climbing back in bed and grasping her hands once more. "Okay," he said. "I trust your discernment on this one. Let's pray."

⌒

The path Cory followed led him to a small church on the other side of the beach. He hadn't attended church in a long time, but he hadn't forgotten the teachings he'd received as a youth. He'd told himself on multiple occasions that he was going to get right with God once his business was at a place where he could take time off to get his spiritual life in order.

It was late at night, but this church was rocking. The music could probably be heard more than a mile away. Cory took it as a sign that God wanted him to return to the church sooner than he'd been planning to. He had just been praying, asking God for help with his love life. So, he figured, why not go into this church and worship the Lord? He couldn't think of one single reason not to. So, he went in.

The choir was throwing down. They sang "Take Me to the King" and then Kirk Franklin's "I Smile." Cory was enjoying himself so much, he reached in his pocket for his cell phone, ready to call Leah and tell her to get over to this church. But then he chided himself for bringing Leah into the mix. He was having an experience with God, and Leah had nothing to do with it. He silently prayed that God would take her out of his thoughts and just allow him to spend some time with his heavenly Father.

When the choir was finished singing, the minister, who introduced himself as Pastor Albury, stood behind the podium and offered a quick word of prayer before inviting everyone to sit. As Cory prepared to hear the message, he was on the edge of his seat. It seemed that whenever he was in church, he never failed to receive direction for his life. He often credited his time in youth group for making him the man he was today. Cory doubted that he would have been able to focus enough to finish college and start a business if the youth pastor hadn't told him all those years ago that God expected him to make something of his life.

It was his youth pastor who'd helped Cory to stop feeling guilty for failing to protect his sister from being killed by her abusive husband.

After that, he'd been empowered to redirect his energy toward discovering all that God had planned for him.

Cory was eager to hear the words that this particular preacher was about to speak into his life.

As Pastor Albury turned the pages of his Bible, he scanned the sanctuary, as if looking for someone. Once he had Cory in his sights, the preacher pointed at him. "Young man."

Cory looked around.

"You," the preacher said, still pointing at him. "Come up here, please. God has a word for you."

Still feeling awful about how she'd treated Cory earlier, Leah put on her nightgown, sat down at the edge of her bed, and pulled her cell phone out of her purse. She saw that her parents' had left her a voice mail, but when she tried to access it, her phone powered off. Leah searched around for her charger but couldn't find it. So, she tucked the phone back in her purse and picked up her novel. She would borrow Brandy's charger in the morning and then give her parents a call.

She stretched out in a lounge chair on her balcony and picked up reading where she'd left off. It would be a helpful diversion—something to take her mind off the friendship she had ruined. She read for about an hour, getting all into the "boy meets girl, boy falls for girl, boy loses girl" plotline as it unfolded in the book, before her eyelids began to droop. The book was good, but she'd had an eventful day, and it was time to shut it down. She returned to her room, got ready for bed, and climbed beneath the covers before turning off the lights.

It didn't take her long to drift off. Soon, she was dreaming—about Cory's captivating smile. He was wearing the straw hat they'd found at the store, but this time, Leah removed it from his head and purchased it for him. And then they left the store, only this time, instead of Cory pressuring her to talk about things she didn't want to discuss, they held hands as they walked down the street. When they reached the car, Cory opened the passenger door for her. Leah hesitated, then put one hand on Cory's face as she used the other to pull him closer.

"What are you up to?" Cory asked her with a grin.

Without answering, she got up on tiptoe and brought her lips to his with a greater abandon than she'd ever exhibited. She'd had to be careful all her life, because men were always trying to take advantage of her. But the ravenous way in which Cory returned the kiss left her feeling spent and undone. Then they pulled apart, breaking the spell. Leah could see him, but she couldn't get to him. No matter what she did, she couldn't get around the barrier that separated them. Cory was her future, but she didn't know how to get to him.

"Calm down, baby. I'm here."

The voice penetrated her dream and caused a chill to run up her spine. She felt the covers being pulled off as someone got in the bed with her. Leah racked her brain, trying to figure out how someone could have gotten into her room. She'd not only locked her door; she'd latched it, as well. But then she remembered that she hadn't locked the door to the balcony when she'd come inside from reading.

"I'm here for what you owe me."

Leah panicked, fully awake now. Had Ned been bailed out of jail and followed her to the Bahamas? But this man didn't sound like Ned.

With a scream, she jumped out of bed, then hit the switch to turn on the light.

"Where are you going, Leah? Don't you believe in paying your debts?"

"You're drunk, Dean, and I don't owe you anything."

"I could have fired you after that screaming fit you pulled in our office, and your boyfriend Cory wouldn't have been able to say a word. But I kept you around, so it's time to pay up." He reached out and grabbed her, pulling her back to the bed.

"Let me go!" she shouted. "Leave me alone!"

But it was no use. He wasn't listening, and he was stronger than his scrawny build had led her to believe.

15

Leon ran like the wind. His charge was in trouble, and he needed to get someone to that hotel room right now. Cory Parker was coming up the walkway to the hotel, having spent the evening being slain in the spirit after receiving the word that God had been trying to get through to him since the day he'd left youth group: "Come home, My son."

Cory had lain on the floor of the church and cried like he had the night he'd discovered that his sister was dead. The experiences were not altogether different, because he'd come to realize that his spiritual life had as good as died, as well. But God was merciful, and He still wanted him. That night, Cory had made up his mind that no matter what he was doing or how far he went in life, he would never forget God again.

Leon was elated for the young man's conversion experience, but now that God had gotten His business with Cory out of the way, Leon needed him to help save Leah. Waving him forward, Leon yelled out to Cory, "Something is wrong with Leah. Hurry. I heard screams coming from her hotel room."

Cory didn't even ask who the man was. As soon as he heard that Leah might be in trouble, he sprinted into the hotel and told the desk clerk, "I need a key to open Leah Davison's door. She's in distress."

"I'm sorry, sir, but I can't give you the key if your name isn't on the room," the man told him.

"Then you'd better follow me with that key, because I'm going to break the door down if I have to."

Knowing the wait for the elevator would waste too much time, Cory opted for the stairs, taking them three at a time. When he reached her floor, he realized that he didn't know which room was hers, so he roamed the halls, listening for sounds of distress and alternately calling her name in ten-second intervals. "Lord, lead me to her," he prayed. "Show me her room."

﹏

"Don't you touch me," Leah yelled as Dean ran his hand down her back.

"That dress you wore tonight was beautiful. Did Ned buy it for you?"

"You're a pig." Wriggling to get away, Leah managed to pull one arm free of his grip. That was when she remembered the pepper spray she had left in the nightstand. She leaned forward, reaching for it. She almost had it when Dean yanked her back toward him.

"Pig or not, you're going to give me what I came here for."

She scratched him with her nails, and he yelped, loosening his grasp enough for her to break free. She opened the drawer and grabbed the pepper spray, and the next time he reached for her, she doused him. And she kept on spraying until he grabbed his eyes and screamed like a little girl.

Her hotel door burst open, and Leah swung around, aiming the canister in that direction. She was fully prepared to spray any newcomers, as well, but it was Cory who rushed in, with a hotel employee right behind him. Leah dropped the spray and rushed into his arms. "Thank you, thank you," she gasped. "How did you know to come help me? And how did you find me?" She couldn't stop shivering.

"I know this is going to sound crazy, but I think it was God. Or an angel. Definitely some divine nudge," Cory told her.

She was trying to process what he'd said when his gaze traveled over her shoulder to Dean, curled up on the mattress with his face in his hands, still whimpering.

"Dean? What on earth are you doing in here?"

"He's drunk, Cory. He attacked me, and...."

"*Attacked* you?" Dean said the words as if nothing could have been further from the truth. "I was simply trying to get what she promised me before we left the States."

Cory looked to Leah. "What is he talking about? Did you promise him sex?"

Cory didn't need to say another word for Leah to know that he was thinking back to that afternoon, when she'd told him that she wouldn't sleep with him in exchange for a diamond bracelet. "I never promised him anything," she insisted. "He's just like all the other men who've tried to insert themselves into my life, thinking they can treat me any way they want."

"She's no better than a prostitute, man," Dean went on, spewing lies. "She offered herself to me in order to get me to let her keep her job."

"Do you want me to call the police, ma'am?" the hotel employee asked Leah.

Completely mortified by the thought of anyone else finding out what Dean had tried to do to her, she turned to Cory. "I don't want to talk to the police tonight. And if they believe Dean over me, I could wind up in prison on foreign soil." She was becoming hysterical at the thought of anyone suspecting her of trying to sell herself.

"Thanks for your help," Cory said to the hotel employee. "I'll let you know if we need anything else."

When the man had left the room, Cory pointed to the door and said, "Get out of here, Dean."

"I can't see enough to go anywhere, man. She got me with pepper spray."

With a look of disgust on his face, Cory turned away from Dean. "Let's get your things together, Leah. We're moving you to an executive suite tonight."

Once Leah's belongings had been transferred to her new suite, she sat on the sofa, trying to settle, while Cory made her a cup of tea to calm her nerves.

The tears that hadn't come during the attack because of the rush of adrenaline were flowing freely now. Cory delivered her tea, then sat down next to her and put an arm around her shoulders. "I'm so sorry about what happened to you, Leah. Tell me what you want me to do, and I'll get it done."

She wanted Dean to pay for what he'd done to her. She wanted Ned to pay, too. But, for that to happen, she would have to be willing to open up to the world about those awful experiences. She kept trying to hide her secrets away in the corners of her mind, hoping they'd get lost there, so that she'd never have to think about them again. But then, someone else did something to her to make her relive the horrors of her life.

"Do you want to talk?" he asked her, handing her a Kleenex.

She took the tissue and wiped the tears from her face. "Where do I start?"

"Wherever you want to. I'm here for you. And if all I can do to help is listen, then I'll do it."

"How about we start with my first real boyfriend—your best friend from high school. The one who dumped me before college. Before he did, he told one of his friends on the football team that he could have me.

"The guy had asked me out on a date before Chris broke up with me, so, of course, I turned him down, since I was already dating some-one. He laughed in my face and told me to guess who had given him my number."

Cory frowned. "I never would have thought Chris would do some-thing like that."

Leah shrugged. "I guess I'm the kind of girl that men think they can treat any kind of way. My sisters managed to find themselves men who treat them like gold, but the only ones I seem to run into are snakes."

"That's not true," Cory said with force behind his tone. "You're a woman that a man should cherish and look after."

"I wish you had asked me out, and well before Chris. I always assumed that you liked me. But when your best friend asked me out instead of you, I figured I had read the signs wrong or something."

Sorrow filled Cory's eyes as he ran his fingers through her hair. "You read the signs right. I was gearing up to ask you out, and Chris knew it, so he made sure to beat me to the punch."

Leah sighed wistfully. "Things would have been so different for me if you had been my boyfriend in high school. Maybe we would have stayed together, huh? And then I never would have taken up with Ned." She exhaled another sigh. "My list of shoulda-coulda-wouldas is so long."

Cory leaned his head against the back of the sofa without responding.

"You don't believe me, do you?"

"I don't want to badger you, Leah. Lord knows you've been through enough tonight. But I don't know what to believe, since you don't want to talk to me about it."

She turned her face away from him. "It's not that I don't want to talk to you. I'm just so tired of reliving this stuff."

Cory sat up again and reached out, turning Leah's face back to him. "The last time I checked, the only perfect person was Jesus Christ. So, this is a no-judgment zone. You can trust me, Leah. I look at you, and I wonder what happened to the bright, vibrant, confident girl I used to dream about. You've changed, and I just wish I knew why."

"But can you handle knowing?" Leah asked. She felt like a broken china doll. She would probably shatter into a thousand pieces if Cory gave up on her now.

He took her hands in his. "I won't let you down. You can trust me."

"I sure hope you're telling the truth." She gulped hard, then began. "I don't know when it happened, but after so many different guys mistreated me, I began believing all men were scum. Except for my dad, that is—I thought he'd hung the moon. But then, one day, I found out that he had a son that none of our family knew about. I became so angry, and I felt that I had to defend my mother against the wrong my father had done. In my rage, I ended up bringing a lot of harm and hurt to my family.

"My father even had a heart attack. That's when we all discovered that my mother had known about my half brother all along. She had been separated from my father at the time when my half brother was conceived, and she had long since made her peace with the incident."

"That had to be tough, discovering that your father had a child you knew nothing about," Cory remarked.

"It was tough," Leah admitted, "but I handled the situation all wrong. I've never confessed to my family the reason I handled things that way, but I'm telling you the truth: I feel as if I've been damaged because of the way men have treated me through the years. Why else would I have dated a creep like Ned?"

"You can't blame yourself for that one," Cory told her. "I was working closely with the man, and I didn't pick up on anything amiss until you came into the conference room and then fled as if you feared someone was trying to kill you."

Leah shivered as she recalled that moment. "I'm tired of talking about Ned and Dean. I want to be free from the evil they have brought to my life." She'd thought about it before, and now it was as clear as ever: she needed to quit. The loss of her job seemed to be the only way to secure her freedom.

When she confided in Cory, he disagreed just as vehemently as he had on her two previous attempts to quit. He stood and began pacing the floor. "You don't have to quit, Leah. Dean attacked you, not the other way around. He's lucky you didn't call the police on him." Cory stopped pacing and turned to her. "Why didn't you call the police?"

"Nobody's going to care what some top-level executive tried to do to his assistant. For all we know, the police would believe his story—that I was trying to sell my body to him."

Cory sat down next to her again. "But you had me and the hotel clerk there to verify your claim. We saw what happened."

Lowering her head, Leah said, "You have your IPO to think about. What would have happened if an executive of your company had been arrested this weekend for attempted rape?"

"I admit that it wouldn't have been good for us. But I'm the CEO and majority holder of the company. I would have figured something out."

"It's not worth all of that," Leah told him. "You've worked too hard to get where you are for someone like me to come along and spoil everything."

"Hey." Cory put a finger under her chin and lifted her face so that she was looking at him when he said, "You're worth so much more than you know. You allowed idiots to convince you that you're worthless. But that's not true. Say the word, and I'll back you with the police. Dean should pay for what he did."

She tried to smile. "Thanks for saying that. Your support means a lot to me. It's encouraging to know that somebody believes me."

"Why don't you believe yourself? That's what I want to know."

Tears welled in her eyes, as she realized that what he had said was true. She didn't think much of herself. And she hadn't for a long time. Her family members were always telling her how special she was, but she couldn't stop seeing them as better than she. Why couldn't she just believe in herself?

"I'm sorry," Cory said. "I didn't mean to make you cry."

She waved off his apology. "It's okay. You're right. I don't think much of myself. It's just that I keep making all the wrong choices. I'm a complete mess." She stood up and wiped the tears from her face. "Do you mind if I take a shower?"

"Not at all. It's time for me to turn in, anyway. But please don't hesitate to call if you need anything—anything at all," he told her.

"Thanks, Cory."

When he'd gone, Leah went into the luxurious bathroom to take a shower. But no matter how hard she scrubbed herself with the aromatherapy bodywash and the loofah, or how long she let the streaming-hot water beat and batter her body, she still felt unclean. Cory had told her that she was worth more than she knew, but it was so hard for her to climb out of the pit she'd dug for herself. So hard for her to imagine that there could be any worth in her. So hard for her to believe that life could get better when it seemed that everywhere she turned, there was a reminder of her worthlessness.

Her brother-in-law had been arrested and now faced criminal charges for trying to defend her against Ned. Now, Cory was willing to throw away his life's work just to defend her honor. She couldn't allow him to do that. She couldn't allow another family member to pay for the problems she'd brought upon herself. It would probably make life easier for her family, for Cory—for everyone—if she wasn't around.

As she got out of the shower, Leah came up with the perfect solution. Life was too hard for her, and she was ready to admit defeat. She took the sleeping pills out of her purse and sat at the edge of her bed, holding the bottle.

Just then, the phone on the nightstand rang.

"You doing okay?" Cory asked when she picked up.

Leah put the pills back in her purse. "Just getting ready to lie down."

"Remember, you let me know if you need anything."

Cory had been good to her. Too good for her to kill herself in this hotel room. She decided that she wouldn't die tonight. But in the morning, Leah would tell Cory that she wanted to explore the island alone. Then she would take a few of her sleeping pills, walk into the surf, and never come back.

16

Cory rose early the next morning after spending the midnight hours in prayer for Leah. She was desperately hurting, and he had no clue how to help her. But as he continued to pray, the Lord had brought to mind the church he'd found. The ministry was having a revival that weekend, with a guest preacher scheduled to speak at the Sunday morning service. Cory hadn't thought much about it when he'd left the church last night, but now he was convinced that God had led him to that church so that he could bring Leah to the service this morning.

He ordered room service for breakfast, then jumped in the shower. Once the food had been delivered, Cory carried the tray down the hall to Leah's suite and knocked on the door. "Breakfast."

"No, thanks," he heard her reply after a short delay. She sounded groggy.

"Well, that's too bad," Cory said. "There's a place I want to take you this morning, and I need you to eat first, because I don't know how long we'll be there."

Leah finally opened the door, still tying the belt of her plush white hotel-supplied bathrobe. "I can't go anywhere with you today, Cory. I have other plans."

"Have a seat." He pointed at the dining table.

Leah didn't argue. She sat down and took the lid off one of the plates. "Mmm, waffles. With strawberries *and* blueberries?"

Cory shrugged. "I didn't know which topping you would prefer, so I went with both."

"Look at you, trying to make me feel all special." She smiled, but Cory noticed that her lips curved up only partway, and her eyes were void of all laughter, as if she had died a little last night.

But he was confident that she would be alright. He had recently become a firm believer in prayer. It worked—God had convinced him of that last night.

"So, what did you have planned for the day?" he asked her.

"I just want to explore the island a little more, that's all." Leah cut into her waffle.

"Sounds like fun. We can do that—"

"No, Cory," she cut him off. "I want to go alone."

Don't argue with her, he coached himself. "I understand. Everyone needs a little alone time once in a while. I had some last night, and I ended up stumbling upon this amazing church near the beach. That's actually the place I want to take you this morning."

Leah scoffed. "I should have known. Of all the teens in our youth group, you seemed like the biggest church boy of them all."

"Hey, my mama raised me right. But, if I recall correctly, you and your sister were in the youth group, too—not to mention that you were the bishop's kids."

"Okay." She grinned, a bit more convincingly this time. "I'll admit to having had fun in youth group."

"Then come with me this morning. I know you've got your own thing planned for the day. But do you think you could hang out with me for two hours first?" His eyes pleaded with her to say yes.

She hesitated a moment. "Oh, fine. How can I say no to a face like yours? Let's finish breakfast, and then I'll get dressed."

~

Once they arrived at the church, and Leah saw how the Spirit of God was moving on everyone around her, she knew she'd made the right decision in joining Cory. This way, he would be able to tell her parents that she had spent the morning of her death at a church, in the presence of a multitude of people who were jumping around shouting praises to the Lord. When they finally pulled her lifeless body out of the ocean, her mother would most certainly say something like, "She's with God now." Leah smiled at the thought. She knew that would bring comfort to her father.

This revival had all the bells and whistles. Fred Hammond and the United Tenors were on stage, singing "Here in Our Praise." Cory was rejoicing, clearly feeling the love of the Savior that the group was singing about. But Leah wasn't feeling much love. She'd grown up in church, but she still didn't understand how people were able to move past their problems and praise God as if nothing else mattered.

After the opening praise and worship, Leah tapped Cory on the shoulder. When he turned to her, she said, "I'm not feeling this. I think I'm just going to leave."

"You came with me. We should leave together. Are you sure you can't just stick it out a little longer? The guest speaker is supposed to be extremely anointed."

"I don't think so," Leah told him. "But don't worry about leaving with me. I'll just catch a cab. It's no big deal."

"You can't just get up and walk out while they're introducing the speaker," Cory whispered, nodding toward the podium. "I know your daddy taught you better than that."

The minister standing at the podium was saying, "First Lady Nina Walker and her husband, Pastor Isaac Walker, are no strangers to this ministry. They have prayed and supported us through the years. Pastor Isaac has preached at our church at least three times, and today, we are truly blessed to have First Lady Nina here to speak to us."

Leah could admit that that would be rude. Her mother and father would be mortified if she were to do something like that at their church, so she decided that she shouldn't disrespect another person's church, either—even if it meant that she'd have to sit through the whole sermon.

"This prayer warrior has been a soldier in the army of the Lord for many years," the minister continued. "You probably weren't aware of the fact that Nina Walker wasn't always saved and sanctified, but she found her way to the Lord. And if you open your heart, you can, too. That's all I'm going to say. I'll let her exhort you with her testimony."

As Nina stepped up to the podium, the congregation stood and clapped.

She nodded with a smile, then invited them to sit before she lifted her head toward heaven and prayed to God, asking Him to bless the congregation and to open the people's hearts to the message He had called her to deliver.

After the prayer, she started paging through the big Bible on the pulpit. "Turn with me, please, to Romans chapter eight. We'll begin reading from verse one:

"There is therefore now no condemnation to them which are in Christ Jesus, who walk not after the flesh, but after the Spirit. For the law of the Spirit of life in Christ Jesus hath made me free from the law of sin and death. For what the law could not do, in that it was weak through the flesh, God sending his own Son in the likeness of sinful flesh, and for sin, condemned sin in the flesh: that the

righteousness of the law might be fulfilled in us, who walk not after the flesh, but after the Spirit."

Nina looked out at the congregation. "You may be asking yourself, *What does all that mean?* I don't know what it means for you, in your particular situation. But, to me, it means that I don't have to condemn myself for the mistakes I've made along the way."

Leah was amazed that the beautiful woman standing behind the pulpit had any flaws at all. She appeared so confident, so take-charge. The more Nina talked, the more Leah soaked up.

"Before Christ came into my life, I had no discernment at all," Nina was saying. "Consequently, I ran after men who were all wrong for me. These men led me into a world of sin that I had no clue how to get out of. I was a dope man's woman. I'd been beaten and left pregnant and alone, with no way to take care of my child.

"But then, one day, Jesus came into my life and showed me that I was worth far more than I gave myself credit for being. He made me realize that I didn't have to permit men to do anything and everything they wanted to do to me. I was a child of God, and that designation carried weight. It demanded respect."

Hadn't Cory said the same thing to her? Leah glanced over at him. He was watching her, as if trying to see if the minister's words were getting through to her. She smiled at him, then turned back to the pulpit.

Nina was now standing in front of the podium with one arm outstretched. "I didn't believe that I was worthy of God's love," she said. "I didn't believe that I was worthy of anyone's love. But then, one day, my Lord Jesus beckoned me to come, and ever since that day, I haven't looked back."

She stepped back behind the pulpit and glanced at her notes before continuing. "I know that some of you are wondering how I have been able to live my life without condemnation since accepting Christ. Some of you are thinking, *Surely, with the kind of life you led, there must be people who try to remind you of your past.*" She looked up and scanned the crowd with a smile. "See? I can read minds."

"And you're right. To this day, the evil one still tries to accuse me with my past. But whenever someone tries to get me down, I remind myself of those bop bags. You know the ones…they're inflatable, and when you hit them, they go down but then pop right back up again. You can't keep one of those bop bags down, and do you know why? Because it's standing up on the inside."

Many of the congregants began to clap enthusiastically, as if her message resonated with them.

"And that's what we all need to do whenever Satan tries to bring guilt and condemnation into our lives—just keep standing up on the inside," Nina said, her pitch rising. "Can I get you to do it now? Come on. Stand up for Jesus. Stand up for the man or the woman you were meant to be."

Without realizing what she was doing, Leah found herself clapping and getting to her feet. She had lived with this feeling of worthlessness long enough.

"And now, I'm going to ask you to take another stand with me," Nina went on. "If you want to know Jesus—the one and only Person who can help you stand against the demonic forces that try to hold you bound— then come down the aisle right now. Come and allow us to pray for you."

Leah hesitated, worrying that if she went down that aisle, others would begin to speculate about why she identified so much with Nina's story. But then she told herself to let go of her foolish worries and get down that aisle to secure what was being freely offered to her.

As she stepped into the aisle and made her way to the front, one of the choir members started singing CeCe Winans' "Alabaster Box." Leah stumbled as her tears blinded her. For the first time in years, she knew without a doubt that she had heard from God.

Nina came down from the pulpit and pointed right at Leah. "It's you," she said. "God sent me here for you."

Leah hardly recognized the feeling of worthiness, of being cherished. Yet that was how she felt, knowing that God had brought Nina Walker all the way to the Bahamas just for her—just because she was important to Him. "Oh, thank You, Jesus," Leah said as she fell into Nina's arms and allowed the woman to minister healing to her soul.

⌒

In the back of the sanctuary, invisible to all human eyes, a host of angels stood watching Leah transform from the caterpillar she once was to the butterfly she would forever be, from now until eternity. They raised their swords and shouted, "Bless the Lord, for He is good!"

Then Leon commanded them to put their swords down. "We need to be vigilant, because I hear our adversary roaring like a lion. He isn't taking this one lying down."

"Well then, let the fight begin," one of the other angels said, lifting his sword again.

17

"I can't thank you enough for bringing me to church this morning," Leah said to Cory as they headed to his rental car after the service. "I feel like God has given me a second chance. I've been born again, for real this time, and it's as if all those terrible things that happened in my past didn't happen to me at all but to the 'me' I used to be." She twirled and danced as they made their way across the parking lot. "My parents aren't going to believe that I rededicated my life to Christ today."

"And just think, you almost left the church before the speaker delivered her message."

"You don't have to rub it in," Leah said, swatting him playfully. "I've been in a bad place for a really long time, and I'm finally feeling good about myself. I don't need anyone trying to bring me down."

Catching a glimpse of the gorgeous ocean waves, Cory put his keys back in his pocket. "Okay, Miss Sunshine. Let's take a walk on the beach, so we can breathe in some of this fresh air and be in awe of what God did for both of us today."

"Sure beats what I had planned for the afternoon."

They looked at each other, losing themselves temporarily in the sweetness of the moment. Then they took off their shoes and tossed them in the car.

Cory clasped Leah's hand and started walking toward the beach. They didn't stop until they reached the water. The waves crashed against the sand, wetting their feet and then gently receding. "I need to tell you something," he said.

She turned and looked at him, beaming. "What is it?"

"I don't know if you even have a clue about this, but I have been in love with you since we were teenagers."

Her brow furrowed in confusion. "What?"

"You heard me."

"But you never said anything. You let me date that jerk friend of yours."

"Nobody told you to say yes to Chris when he asked you out. You could have waited for me to get up the nerve."

She grinned. "You were nervous? I can't believe that Cory Parker was scared of a girl. I mean, you seemed very confident while you were dating half the cheerleading squad."

"Only because I couldn't have you, remember? None of those relationships lasted. And now I know why." He reached up and gently rubbed the side of her face. "You're the only woman for me, Leah. I want to spend the rest of my life loving you. I just wish you would give me the chance."

Cory's hand felt warm and good on her face. His words had penetrated her heart with happiness. But fear crept in and stole the moment.

"Please don't do this now," Leah told him. "I have to be honest with you: Love has never been something I excelled at. And right now, the only love I can trust is the one I found at church this morning."

"You can trust me."

She closed her eyes as a tear slid down her face. "I want to trust you, Cory. I want to drop my defenses and love you with all that is in me. But I've been so wrong before...so many times."

Inching closer to her, he said, "You're not wrong about me."

Could she take a chance at love with Cory? He seemed like everything she'd ever wanted. But could she trust herself to make the right decision about a man on the heels of everything that had happened with Ned and then with Dean?

She needed time. Needed to pray. And she opened her mouth to tell Cory as much, but before she could utter a word, he had captured her mouth with his.

The kiss was divine. It was magical. Leah didn't want it to end. But if she was ever going to have any hope of getting it right with a man, she needed to have her wits about her when she prayed. So, as the water caressed their feet again, she moved away from the heat of his embrace. "We can't."

"Please don't push me away like this," he pleaded.

"Give me some time, Cory. I need to pray about this." She desperately needed him to understand. "I know that you're a good guy. But I can't commit my heart to you when I'm still dealing with unresolved issues."

"I understand," he said. But the look in his eyes didn't mesh with his words.

Leah touched his arm. "I meant what I said last night—that if I had dated you in high school, my life would have been a lot different. I'm tired of connecting with the wrong people and making misguided decisions about relationships. And that means I need to be a lot more careful—and a lot more prayerful—with future relationships."

"I'm not going to pressure you," Cory said, holding up his hands and slowly backing away. "But will you at least allow me to take you to lunch? I'm sure you're hungry again by now."

"I'm starving," Leah admitted.

"Let's head back to the car and go get something to eat."

As they got into the car, Leah looked at Cory with a mischievous grin. "I'll even let you pay."

"Oh, thanks for thinking of me. You're so considerate. Let me get out my GPS so I can find the nearest McDonald's."

Punching his arm playfully, Leah said, "Hey, I just rededicated my life to Christ, buster. Your old youth group buddy deserves better than a burger and fries on a day like today."

"Didn't you hear? McDonald's has come up in the world. They're serving chicken wings now."

"Whatever. I just know you better not pull up at a place with golden arches."

They continued their good-natured banter as they drove along. Then Cory told her, "I'm just joking with you, woman. I'm taking you to Seafire Steakhouse. It's some of the best dining the resort has to offer."

"That sounds much better. You just earned two cool points back."

When they stepped inside the restaurant, Leah decided he'd earned an extra cool point. "This place is beautiful," she told him breathlessly.

"I thought you might like it."

They took their seats and wasted no time placing their orders.

"I'm so hungry, I could eat everything on the menu," Cory said.

"I feel the same way," Leah told him. "Being at church this morning really drained me, but in a good way. You know what I mean?"

"I know exactly what you mean." Then Cory told her about his experience the night before.

"And you just happened upon this church?"

Cory thought about that for a moment. "I can't say that for sure. I remember being on the beach last night, feeling sorry for myself, and then it was as if this path appeared that I felt compelled to follow."

"Thank God for obedience," Leah said with a nod. "But I hope I wasn't the reason you were feeling sorry for yourself."

"I'm not going to lie—you were part of the reason. But I received a call from the new financial consultant yesterday, and he thinks we have a problem that might hold up the IPO."

"Oh, really?" Leah leaned forward. "Do you want to talk about it? I mean, I don't want to pry if it's not something you're at liberty to discuss."

He waved her concern away. "It's no big deal. Plus, I think this new guy has made an error in his calculations. He's telling me that the company owes two million more on the building than it's worth. There's no way that can be, so I'll just take care of it when we get back to the States."

"And a mistake like that could stop you from going public?"

"I don't know if it would stop the process. But we would have to disclose, which might make it look as if we're not responsible with our money…and that would be all bad. But I'm sure we will be able to clear this up, so I'm trying not to worry about it. And the service this morning really helped take it off my mind."

"Good." Leah nodded. "You need to relax. You've worked so hard to make your dreams come true, and I'm praying it all goes off without a hitch. That's why I figured it would be best if I just let this issue with Dean go."

Cory scowled. "I don't want to talk about Dean. He should be arrested for what he pulled with you. I want you to seriously consider reporting him to the authorities."

"But I don't want to mess things up for you." Then Leah remembered something she'd been meaning to tell Cory. "There was this document that I asked Dean about—"

"No discussion about Dean. Not today, okay?"

"But I really think you should know this."

"Then tell me tomorrow. I just want to enjoy the rest of the day. We'll be on a plane headed back to reality tomorrow. So, let's forget about IPOs and business partners for one day." Smiling at her and putting his hand over hers, he added, "Just let me be with you today."

"How can I deny your request when you ask like that?"

When they'd finished their meal, they went back outside for some fresh air. Cory offered Leah his arm, and she took it with a smile, enjoying being treated with such chivalry. Her radar had made her wary before, but she felt confident now that Cory was a good guy; she just needed to discover if he was the right guy for her.

She wasn't left with much time to think about it, though, because as they were crossing the road nearest the restaurant, a car came barreling at them from out of nowhere. Leah tried to pull Cory toward her, but once he saw the car, he pushed her in the opposite direction, out of the way. Before he could make it to safety, the car connected with his body and knocked him to the ground.

"No!" Leah screamed, running toward him.

The car skidded to a stop, made a reverse turn, and sped away.

When she reached Cory, Leah fell down on her knees beside him. His eyes were closed, and he wasn't moving. She lifted his head into her lap. "Wake up, Cory. Please, wake up."

Her eyes filled with tears as she looked around for somebody, anybody. "Help us! Somebody, please help!" she screamed while sobbing uncontrollably.

Cory wouldn't wake up. How could this be happening?

"Don't you die on me," she told him, rocking him in her arms.

18

"What color was the car?" the police officer asked.

"I don't know, exactly," Leah said. "It was dark. Black, maybe. Or hunter green." She kept looking around the hospital waiting room, her eyes darting every direction, as if she were lost and trying to figure out how she'd gotten there.

"Did you see the driver?"

"It all happened so fast, I barely saw anything. But I didn't need to. I know who did it."

"You have a name for me?"

She nodded. "Dean Richards. Last night, he broke into my hotel room and tried to rape me. This time, he was trying to run me over with his car, but Cory pushed me out of the way and got hit, instead." Wiping the tears from her eyes with some tissue, she added, "I want to press charges." She was no longer worried about what others might think. Her family had stopped keeping secrets a long time ago, and it was time for her to do the same. She had given her life to Christ, and she was standing up on the inside now. Never again would she sit back passively while others did whatever they wanted to do to her.

"You say that this man tried to rape you?"

"Yes. He came in through the balcony door. I have two witnesses— Cory and the hotel employee who caught Dean in my room. Fortunately, I had a canister of pepper spray nearby and was able to use it to hold him off."

The officer asked Leah a series of other questions. As they were wrapping up the interview, the emergency room doors swung open, and a nurse emerged. Leah got to her feet. "How's he doing?"

"He's pretty banged up," the nurse admitted. "But we can't get him settled because he won't stop asking for you. Can you come back for a few minutes, just so he can see that you're okay?"

Turning toward the police officer, Leah said, "He needs me."

"Go on," the officer told her. "I'll file the paperwork and bring it back for you to sign."

Leah followed closely behind the nurse, anxious to see Cory for herself. When they arrived at his room, Leah rushed inside and sat in the chair beside his bed. "Oh, Cory, thank goodness. I was so worried. How are you feeling?"

He grimaced but then managed a grin. "I think I may have a few cracked ribs, but I can't tell you how good it is to see your face. I must have passed out or something, because I had no clue what had happened to you."

"You pushed me out of the way."

"I did?"

She nodded. "If it wasn't for you. I'd be lying in a bed in the room next door. You're such a good man, Cory Parker. I'm so thankful that you are in my life—not to mention that you saved my life."

"You're just saying that because I'm all banged up," he joked.

Just then a doctor came in. "It looks like you'll be here overnight for observation," he told Cory.

Cory started to object but ended up biting his lower lip, clearly hurting too much to speak.

"We'll get you something for the pain, too."

"When?" Cory gasped.

"A nurse is bringing it now," the doctor said, then left the room.

"I hate that you're in so much pain," Leah told him. "I should be the one lying in that hospital bed."

Cory shook his head. "Don't say things like that," he admonished her. "Even with the pain I'm in, I would be devastated if that car had hit you instead of me."

Another nurse came in with Cory's medicine. After he'd taken it, he turned back to Leah. "What I'm wondering is, why on earth that car came at us like that in the first place."

"I told the police that I was certain it was Dean. I also told them that I wanted to press charges against him for attacking me last night." Leah held her breath, wondering how Cory would take the news that she had just thrown a monkey wrench in his IPO plans. She no longer cared what anyone might think of her, even if all the dirty details of her relationship with Ned came out. But she needed Cory to be on her side.

"I'm glad you told the police about what Dean did to you. But I don't think he would have tried to run us down. He needs me alive to finish this IPO."

Leaning back in her seat, Leah said, "Sometimes, I wonder if Dean even cares if this IPO goes through or not."

"Oh, believe me, he cares," Cory assured her. "He likes money just as much as the next person." His eyelids fluttered—clearly, the pain pills were beginning to take effect. "Don't go back to the hotel without me tonight," he told her. "Ask the nurse to bring in an extra bed or a reclining chair."

"If you don't think Dean would have tried to run us down, then why are you so worried about my going back to the hotel?" Leah asked.

"I don't know, exactly, but there's too much funny business going on. I don't want anything to happen to you." He held out a hand to her. "I feel myself starting to drift off. Promise me that you'll stay with me tonight. I couldn't bear to lose you. I was so terrified when the police found that gun in Ned's car, and then someone tried to run you down. Just stay here, okay?"

Leah squeezed his hand. "I promise. Now, get some sleep. I won't go anywhere. Besides, I need to tell you about some files I found in Dean's office. But we can talk in the morning."

Within minutes, Cory was snoring, and Leah was standing over him, watching while he slept. "Thank You, Lord," she prayed. "Thank You for keeping him alive."

Leah hadn't eaten a thing since lunch, and it was now close to eleven at night. Fortunately, the hospital cafeteria was still open. She purchased a sandwich and some chips. On her way back across the main lobby, she ran into the police officer who'd questioned her earlier.

"How is your friend?" he asked as he walked up to her.

"He's resting."

"Good. I brought the complaint for you to sign."

Leah looked the document over, then signed it. She felt good about finally doing something—taking action—rather than just allowing awful things to happen to her.

The automatic doors of the hospital opened, and Leah glanced over to see Dean Richards strolling in.

"That's him," she said, pointing in his direction.

"Who? Where?"

"Dean Richards. He just walked in." She pointed again. "He's standing at the information desk."

The officer strode over to Dean. "Dean Richards?"

Dean turned to the officer. "Yes, that's me. Do you have any news about my business partner?"

The officer took out his handcuffs. "You'll need to come with me."

"What are you talking about?" Dean asked, frowning. "I can't go with you. I need to check on my partner."

"Ms. Leah Davison has filed a complaint against you for breaking into her hotel room and attacking her," the officer informed him.

"You're not getting anywhere near Cory after you tried to kill us," Leah spat in Dean's face.

"Step back, ma'am," the officer told her. "I'm taking care of this."

"What is she talking about?" Dean demanded as the officer fastened the handcuffs around his wrists. "I didn't do anything to them."

"Oh, I'm sure you didn't do it, just like you didn't sneak into my hotel room and attack me last night."

"You wanted me," Dean shouted back as he was ushered out of the hospital. "You sell it for a living. And now you're lying to cover up the fact that you're a whore."

Leah was thankful that Dean had been taken into custody, but she couldn't believe the lies he kept spewing about her. She wanted to run after him and scratch his eyes out, but then they'd both be going to jail.

Still, she needed to get those words out of her head. So, when she returned to Cory's hospital room, she pulled out her iPhone, ready to play some uplifting music or to look up some Scriptures. That's when she remembered that she had forgotten to charge her phone. She went out to the nurses' station and thankfully found a nurse who was willing to lend her a charger.

Leah leaned back in the recliner in the corner of Cory's room and stretched her legs out on the footrest, trying to relax. But the moment her phone was charged enough to come alive again, it started dinging incessantly, alerting her to all the calls and text messages she'd missed. She popped up out of the chair and grabbed it. There were several text messages from her parents and her sisters telling her to call them right away.

With all that had been going on, Leah couldn't believe that she had neglected to call her parents. Then again, she knew exactly why she hadn't thought to call. She was embarrassed about what Dean had attempted to do. She hadn't wanted to tell her parents that her boss had tried to rape her. Would they assume that she had promised him sex so she'd be included on the trip, as Dean had basically implied? She had made so many poor judgment calls, and she just didn't want her family to think she was still making one mistake after another.

Yes, she had made mistakes, but not everything was her fault. And God was not bringing these disasters on her to pay her back for what she'd done to her father. Her heavenly Father and her earthly father had both forgiven her, and that was that. She picked up her cell phone and called her parents.

"Leah!" her mother exclaimed when she picked up. "We've been so worried about you."

"I forgot to charge my cell phone, Mama," she explained. "I'm sorry that I didn't think to call you sooner."

"We've all been praying for you. The Lord woke me up last night, and I just couldn't shake the feeling that you were in grave danger," her mother told her.

Leah was so thankful that her parents were believers who actually paid attention to the things of God. Where would she be right now if they hadn't been attuned to the Spirit's guidance and hadn't prayed for her?

"I really needed those prayers, Mama," she admitted. "I hate to tell you this, but I'm sick of keeping secrets." She took a deep breath. "My boss broke into my hotel room last night and tried to rape me."

"What?" her mother shouted. "Now, Leah, I know that you're a grown woman, but I demand that you come home right now."

Leah started crying. "I wish I could leave right now, Mama. But then, this afternoon, my boss tried to run me down with his rental car, and he ended up hitting Cory."

"Cory? Oh, Lord Jesus, help us all," her mother murmured. "How is Cory doing? Is he all right? Did he have to go to the hospital?"

"Yes, Mama. That's why I can't leave. We're at the hospital now, and they're keeping him overnight. Cory's in a lot of pain, and I can't just abandon him. Especially since he saved me from Dean—both last night and this afternoon."

"I just want you out of there," her mother told her.

"I know, Mama. And I promise you that as soon as Cory is able to travel, I will be on the first plane that's headed your way."

"I don't know how I feel about that, Leah. Isn't there anyone else who can stay there with Cory?"

"Of course, there is. But I'm not about to leave him in anyone else's care. It's the least I can do to show my gratitude for all he's done for me." She could scarcely believe how possessive she'd suddenly become of Cory. But no one was going to harm him again—not on her watch.

"Cory didn't just save me from Dean, Mama. I was feeling really depressed after the incident, along with the whole situation with Ned, and I just wanted to die. But Cory took me to this little church right off the beach for their service this morning, and the words of the guest speaker ministered to my soul. I gave my heart back to the Lord today, and I have Cory to thank."

"Oh, praise God…praise God!" her mother exclaimed, over and over.

Leah noticed Cory move slightly, and she feared that her phone conversation might be disturbing his sleep. "I've got to go, Mama," she said. "But please tell Daddy and everyone else that I love them. I'm so grateful to have a family like ours."

"Call me first thing in the morning," her mother admonished her.

"First thing," Leah repeated, then ended the call.

After speaking to her mother, Leah felt better. But that still hadn't taken away the sting of Dean's comments. She needed something to calm the raging storm brewing inside of her. So, she downloaded a free app that loaded the King James Version of the Bible on her phone. Then she propped her feet up again and started reading. The Word of God concerning condemnation had brought her peace earlier today. She decided to search the Scriptures to discover who God said she was, so that she would no longer listen to the words running through her head from those who intended to hurt her and cause her to doubt her worth.

She stayed awake until the early-morning hours, soaking up Bible verses that told her she was more than a conqueror through Christ and that reminded her that though the righteous may fall, the Lord was able to deliver them.

By morning, Dean's words no longer had the power to hurt her or to damage her sense of self-worth. She knew that she was a child of the King, and that was all that mattered.

19

Leah had finally drifted off, and when she awakened, she had a crick in her neck from sleeping in that chair. She stood up and stretched every part of her body, thinking that she would have her mother schedule another girls' day of massages as soon as she returned home.

After the doctor had come in to check on Cory, he told him, "I'll be putting in your release papers, so you should be able to leave in a couple of hours."

"Thanks," Cory said. "I no longer feel like I've been run over by a train, so that's progress, right?"

When the doctor had gone, Leah told Cory, "I'm going to head back to the hotel and get you a change of clothes."

He shook his head. "I don't want you going near that hotel without me."

"It's okay," she assured him. "Dean came to the hospital last night, and he was taken into custody."

"You had him arrested?" Cory sat up quickly, then grimaced. "I wish you had talked to me before doing that."

"I'm worth more than I know...remember when you said that to me?"

Cory ran his hand over his face. "Okay, you're right. You should have called the police the other night. I'll stand with you on this."

"Are you sure you're with me, Cory? Because if you need to get behind Dean so that your IPO will go over smoothly, I'll understand."

"I said I'm with you," he snapped. He softened his voice to add, "You may not believe it, but you're worth more to me than ten thousand IPOs."

"Okay, then." She smiled. "I'll go get your toiletries and a change of clothes."

"Hurry back," Cory told her.

When Leah's cab pulled up at the Atlantis, the rest of the Pro-Site staff were standing out front with their luggage, waiting on the airport shuttle.

"Oh, thank God!" Brandy said when she saw Leah. "Everyone's been worried sick about you and Cory and Dean. I was beginning to think that someone had kidnapped all of y'all."

"No kidnapping, but Cory did get hit by a car. He's in the hospital."

"Why didn't you call us?"

"I'm sorry, Brandy. I should have called, but I wasn't thinking straight."

"What about Dean?" Larry asked as he approached them.

Leah didn't want to get into what had happened with Dean, so she said, "I saw him at the hospital last night. He's probably going to be sticking around for another few days."

"Yeah, you're right," Brandy said. "I'm sure Dean wouldn't want to leave without Cory."

"Well, I'll see you all back at home in a few days," Leah told them. "Hopefully, it won't be a problem for us to change our plane tickets for the next available flight."

Then she went inside and headed for the elevators. As she made her way to Cory's suite, she reflected on the events of the day before and felt more certain than ever that it was Dean who had hit Cory. None of the other staff members had known what had happened to her and Cory. How else would Dean have known to look for them at the hospital, unless he was the one who had put them there?

Dean was such a creep. Leah was glad that she wouldn't be working for him anymore. She would miss the job, but it was time for her to start pursuing a real career. What was the purpose behind all those years of college and grad school—and all that tuition money—if not for her to spread her wings and soar? She planned on updating her résumé the moment she returned home.

After stopping in Cory's suite for the items he'd requested, she decided to grab a few things from her own room. As she rummaged around in her suitcase, she was humming the lyrics to "Praise Is What I Do." She caught herself and started laughing. When had she become a praiser?

"I don't see anything funny about this situation," said a voice that sent a chill down her spine. "You kept me waiting here all night. I wonder how you're going to make that up to me."

∾

"Did you reach Leah?" Alma asked her husband as he came into the kitchen.

"No. She's not answering her cell, and I've left several messages in her hotel room." He sat down at the kitchen counter. "Is she going to get on that plane today or not?"

Shaking her head, Alma set David's breakfast in front of him, then grabbed her cell phone and dialed Leah's number. The call immediately went to her voice mail, so Alma waited for the beep and then said, "Hey, honey. We were just calling to check on you. Can you give us an update on when you'll be flying home? Thanks." After hanging up, she turned to David again. "I don't feel right about this."

"Let's put out a few more calls," David suggested. He picked up the house phone and called Solomon.

When he picked up, David put him on speakerphone. "Hi, Son. You haven't heard from Leah, by any chance, have you?"

"Not since she left for the Bahamas," Solomon replied. "Why? What's going on?"

"I'm not sure. We haven't been able to get ahold of her all morning. Alma finally spoke to her yesterday evening, but the things she learned from Leah kept her up praying for the second night in a row. She promised she would call us this morning. But, so far, nothing."

"That's not like Leah," Solomon said. "She's usually good about keeping in touch."

"That's why we're concerned."

"Did you call the hotel?"

"We called there this morning," David confirmed. "They said that she'd been moved to a different room, but even they couldn't reach her."

"There's something I need to tell you, Dad." Solomon took a deep breath. "I was going to call you later today to let you know: According to one of my business associates, Ned made bail on Saturday."

"They let that monster out already?" David exclaimed. "What a joke the justice system is."

"There's something else," Solomon said. "Jonathan said that his accountant has discovered money missing from his business investment account. They think Ned stole the money. So, Jonathan is planning on filing a police report."

"Thanks for telling me, Son. I think I know what I need to do now." David pressed the button to end the call, his shoulders slumping in a show of defeat. "I feel so powerless, Alma," he said with a sigh. "Our daughter needs us, but she's too far away for us to help right now."

"But we know Someone who can help her far better than we could ever hope to." Reaching out, she took his hand in hers and gave it a squeeze. "Come, my love. Come with me to my prayer room. Remember, where two or three are gathered together in God's name, He will be there in their midst. I'm trusting Him to bring Leah back to us."

Dropping the clothes she had been pulling out of her suitcase, Leah stood and turned around to face her worst nightmare.

"Imagine my surprise when I discovered that you traveled all the way to the Bahamas to sleep with your boss," Ned snarled, inching toward Leah. "And you act as if I'm nothing because of one little mistake."

"I didn't sleep with Dean. You're insane."

She should have been trembling with fear, but she wasn't. Not when she knew God was on her side. And she'd never needed Him more.

"I'm not talking about Dean, nitwit. You think I didn't know that you had your hooks in Cory when he fired me?"

"I don't have hooks in Cory, or in anybody else."

"That's right. Because Cory told me how he plans to use you and then throw you away like the trash you are."

"You're a liar!"

"How do you know?"

"Because I've known Cory since grade school. He's a gentleman. He's nothing like you."

"Keep talking, and I'll smack you in that stupid mouth of yours."

"Why are you still following me around if I'm trashy and stupid?" Leah demanded, running on faith-fueled adrenaline. "One would think you'd find a better way to spend your time. But you evidently have nothing better to do. Business not going so well? Is that why you have so much free time?"

He grabbed a handful of her hair and pushed her down on the ground. "Say that you love me, Leah," he roared. "Tell me how much."

But Leah wasn't intimidated by him—not anymore. She shook her head. "I found love this weekend, so I finally know what real love is. And I could never feel that way about you."

Anger etched deep furrows in Ned's face, and he slapped her.

Leah's head snapped back, but she raised it again like one of those bop bags Nina Walker had preached about. She smiled as she reminded herself to keep standing up on the inside. "Is that all you've got?" she sassed him. "My sister used to hit me harder than that when we were in grade school."

"How dare you talk to me like that!" Ned sputtered.

She stood to her feet and got in his face. "Get used to it, Ned. I'm not afraid of you anymore."

"You think your lover-boy Cory Parker will keep you safe from me?"

"I wasn't talking about Cory. I'm in love with my Lord and Savior, Jesus Christ. And His love is greater than all the evil you possess."

As she said these words to him, Leah was silently praying to God, telling Him that she wanted to live. Asking Him to rescue her from Ned. But she also told Him, "However, if I am to join You in Paradise this very day, then that's all right, too. I just thank You for saving me."

Ned reached into his jacket and pulled out a gun. "This is what I possess." He shook the weapon in her face. "And if you keep talking like that, you're going to get one of these bullets between your eyes."

That didn't sound painless, so Leah shut her mouth. But she kept up her silent prayers.

"Nothing to say, huh? All that talk about Jesus has gone out the window now that you see what I'm working with." He waved the gun in the air. "Go on, call out to Jesus. See if He can deliver you from my wrath."

She didn't respond but only kept sending unspoken prayers heavenward.

"Go on, call Him!" he taunted her.

"My God is able to deliver me," she finally said. "I believe that with all my heart."

"Then you're a bigger fool than I ever imagined." He raised the gun and held the barrel against her temple. "Aren't you?"

"No."

"You've got to the count of three to let me hear you say that you are a fool."

He started counting.

But Leah was not moved. She had resolved never to think less of herself than God had called her to think. She would go to her grave knowing God's love and His peace, but she would never again say anything about herself that God hadn't said.

"The Word of God tells me that I am fearfully and wonderfully made," she declared. "I'm not a fool. I'm not stupid or worthless or any other name you can think to call me. I'm a child of God, and that means something."

Sputtering from anger, he lifted the butt of the gun and slammed it down on the crown of her head.

⌐

"How many demons are in there with them?" Leon asked Stephen.

"It's a room full of 'em, and the more Leah talks about God, the rowdier they get. We need to do something, and fast. I'm not sure how much longer she can stand against Ned's assaults."

"We need to get Cory here so he can take care of Ned while we go to war with his demons."

"I'm on it," Stephen said as he disappeared.

⌐

Cory was leaning on the "call nurse" button like an addict needing a fix. Something had happened to Leah—he just knew it. And he had to get out of this hospital so he could go find her.

The nurse came into the room, shaking her head. "Can you please get your finger off that buzzer? We already gave you your pain medicine and your breakfast."

"I want my release papers," Cory told her firmly.

"Just hold on. We're working on them. You'll be out of here soon enough." As she stormed out of the room, Cory heard her mutter, "Believe me, nobody wants you out of here sooner than we do."

"Soon enough" wasn't good enough for Cory. His ribs had been taped, and his back was still hurting, but he somehow found the strength to pull off the covers and get out of the hospital bed. He found his clothes folded on the chair next to the bed. The shirt he'd worn to church yesterday was splattered with blood. He put it on, anyway, then moaned and groaned as he bent down to put on his pants and then his shoes.

⌒

As Cory left the room, Stephen went ahead of him, waving his sword to and fro. He felt the demonic forces approaching, and he was ready to slay any of them who dared to get in their way.

20

I have your sister," Ned told Jonathan, using his cell phone on speaker, since he had Leah bound and gagged.

"I want to speak to her," Jonathan said.

"And I want you to inform the police that I didn't steal anything from you," Ned told him. "Everything I took was payment for my services."

"Let me speak to Leah!"

"First, let's talk about the payment for my services."

"You stole half a million dollars from our investment fund. If I hadn't fired you, who knows how much more you would have taken?"

"If you hadn't fired me, I would have been able to put the funds back."

"That's what all thieves say. How about not taking money that doesn't belong to you? Then you wouldn't have to worry about putting it back. Now, let me speak to Leah!"

Ignoring his demand, Ned said, "I not only want you to take back all your lies, but I also need two million. I want it wired to an account in the Bahamas, and I want it by the end of the business day today."

"I'm not doing anything until I've spoken with Leah," Jonathan maintained.

Ned reached over and peeled the duct tape off Leah's mouth. In spite of the stinging pain, Leah didn't scream but said calmly, "Don't give him anything, Jonathan. Don't put your business in jeopardy for this slime."

"Leah! Thank God. I can't just leave you in his hands," Jonathan said.

"*Trust* God," she told him. "And be sure to let Mama and Daddy know that my trust is in the Lord, too, so I'm good. Do you hear me? I'm okay with however this turns out. God's will be done."

Ned pressed the tape over her lips again. "I have her tied up with a gun to her head," he snarled. "Does that sound okay to you? I doubt that your pretty little wife would want you to sit there and do nothing to help her sister."

"Please don't hurt her," Jonathan pleaded.

"Get me my money."

"Okay, but I don't have that kind of cash lying around. I wouldn't be able to wire the money until tomorrow, at the earliest."

"Then I guess you'd better work your magic." Ned hung up the phone, then peeled the tape off Leah's mouth once more.

"Why can't you leave my family out of this?" Leah pleaded with him. "They have nothing to do with us." Her hands and feet were still tied to a bedpost, but she didn't need her hands and feet to fight Ned. Leah's weapons of choice were prayer and praise.

"Jonathan has everything to do with us. Why do you think I asked you out in the first place? I was only trying to get in good standing with his corporation. And then you suddenly decided that you didn't want to go out with me anymore. You've been getting in my way from the very beginning, and that's why I had to punish you."

Just knowing Ned had been punishment enough. She was almost relieved to discover that he hadn't genuinely liked her in the first place, and that he'd been terrorizing her simply because she'd thwarted his schemes.

She decided not to respond, though, because Ned was clearly unstable, and it looked as if he was coming completely unglued right before her eyes.

She hadn't taken the time to memorize many Scriptures, but when she was in high school, the entire youth group had been challenged to memorize the Twenty-third Psalm. Back then, she couldn't imagine a situation where knowing the Twenty-third Psalm would come in handy, but she was sure glad she'd accepted the challenge.

She began reciting it aloud: "'*The* LORD *is my shepherd; I shall not want. He maketh me to lie down in green pastures: he leadeth me beside the still waters. He restoreth my soul: he leadeth me in the paths of righteousness for his name's sake. Yea, though I walk through the valley of the shadow of death, I will fear no evil: for thou art with me'*—"

"Shut up!" Ned screamed at her.

⌢

When Jonathan called, Alma put him on speakerphone.

"Mom? Dad? Ned has Leah. He wants me to wire him two million dollars by the end of the business day today for him to let her go." Jonathan's voice sounded shaky, timorous.

Alma grabbed the edge of the kitchen counter to steady herself, as David collapsed into a chair, looking almost as faint as he did the day of his heart attack.

"The blood of Jesus," Alma said. "Father, we need You."

"There's something else," Jonathan said, sounding despondent. "Leah wanted me to tell you that her trust is in God, and that she's okay...however this may resolve."

Tears flowed out of Alma's eyes as she turned to her husband. "Our prayers have been answered, David," she told him. "God is with her. We don't have to worry."

"I believe that God is with her," David said, "but I still want my baby girl back home. Can you go online and order two plane tickets to the Bahamas?"

"Of course," Alma told him. "Jonathan? We'll need you to call the rest of the family and tell them to pray like never before. David and I are going to the Bahamas to bring our child back. The devil can't have what God has blessed us with."

⌇

Nina Walker and her husband, Isaac, had just returned home from their trip to the Bahamas and were unpacking their suitcases when Nina stopped cold. "Something is wrong," she said.

"The kids are fine, hon," her husband told her. "I promise you, everything is good with the Walker family."

"I'm not talking about our children." She sat down on the edge of the bed. "Do you remember that girl I prayed for at church on Sunday?"

"The one that you said you believed God had sent you to the Bahamas for?"

Nina nodded. "She reminded me so much of myself at her age. I was so insecure and broken that I allowed other people to take advantage of me, doing things that no person should have to endure. When that young lady came down the aisle, God showed me the things she had suffered. She was freed from all that when she allowed the precious blood of Jesus to wash her clean."

"But you're still feeling a burden for her?" Isaac asked, sitting down next to his wife.

"Yes. I can't explain it, but I see her in a very dangerous battle that could cost her everything. I think we should pray for her, and also get a prayer chain started."

"Okay," Isaac agreed. "I'll call the leader of our intercessory prayer team and ask her to get the chain going on our end."

After making the necessary phone calls, Nina and Isaac came back together and got on their knees to pray. Isaac began. "Heavenly Father, we thank You for Your grace and mercy. We praise You because of how You have changed us and made us new. We praise You for doing the same for our dear sister Leah, and we come to You now, asking that You would protect her. Send Your warrior angels to do battle on her behalf. From whatever danger, seen or unseen, that now threatens her, we ask that You would make a way of escape for her…."

～

"Why don't you just go on and shoot me?" Leah asked Ned.

"Because I want my money," Ned answered simply. "Do you think I enjoy what I'm doing? I don't want to hurt you."

Leah chuckled. "They caught you at my office with a gun, remember?"

"It wasn't for you." He sat down on the bed and touched the side of her face with his fingertips.

She turned away, but she couldn't escape his reach.

"You really are beautiful," he told her. "I know I said that I dated you just to get to your brother-in-law's money, but I still think that we would be good together. If you would just work with me, I'd gladly take you with me."

Did he think she was Boo Boo the fool? Ned had done nothing but torment her. Her life had become a nightmare. She'd even contemplated killing herself because of all that he had done to her. And he had the audacity to ask her to work with him? She'd sooner spit on his grave than agree to such a thing. She knew full well that Christians were supposed to forgive and let things go, but she was new at this thing.

"You can't do it, can you?" Ned stood up with the saddest look she'd ever seen on his face. "You hypocrite. You sit there, praying to God and quoting Scripture, but you won't forgive me for one little fight."

"Little fight"? The man was crazy. She turned away, not able to face him. He had her tied up, and still he had the audacity to ask something of her—something as costly as forgiveness. No, she couldn't do it. Not now, at least. He would be burning in hell before she even thought about forgiving him.

"You did me so wrong," she told him. "I never hurt you. I just didn't want to date you anymore. But instead of letting it go, you tortured me."

"Costing my company business does hurt me. If I don't have cash flow coming in, how do you expect me to pay my bills? Or don't you worry about such things?" Ned stared at her, appearing confounded. "It's not like I wanted to hit you that night. But I was so angry that you were messing up my plans. I knew that if Jonathan saw us as a couple, it wouldn't be long before I was managing his accounts on a permanent basis."

"You were stealing from Jonathan. How could you think he'd never find out?"

"I borrowed that money," Ned insisted. "And if I would have had enough time to work things out, I would have returned it. But you wouldn't give me a chance."

"You attacked me, Ned. How on earth could you have expected me to ever give you another chance?"

"You're such a crybaby. 'You attacked me,'" Ned said, mimicking her in a high-pitched voice. Then he exploded. "What about me? What about the fact that a man's self-worth comes from his earning potential, and I was losing contracts right and left? But that means nothing to you, does it?"

She looked him dead in the eye and said, "I care about my dignity. You took that from me when you attacked me and kept stalking me. You made me doubt my own self-worth. And for that, I hate you."

"Isn't hate a sin?"

He'd struck a nerve with that one. What if her unresolved hatred of Ned was the only sin that kept her from making it to heaven? She prayed for enough time left on earth to find a way to forgive Ned, because today certainly wasn't the day.

"How you dare talk to me about forgiveness, after everything you've done?" Leah lashed out. "You're despicable and evil, and I do hate you, sin or not. Dear God, help me, but I hate him so much." Tears rolled down her face as the hatred she felt seemed to wrap itself around her and refused to let go.

⟜

Long black tentacles massaged Leah's brain with messages of hate. "That's right," the demon whispered. "Remember everything he did to you. Remember everything that every man you trusted ever did to you. Don't ever stop hating Ned. He did you wrong."

Leon strode into the room and drew his sword. "Let her go," he commanded the demon. He had been preparing himself for this battle and was determined that Leah would not lose the faith she had recently discovered due to the infiltration of demonic hate.

"This is none of your business," the demon told him.

"Oh, it's my business." Leon pointed to Leah and said, "She belongs to the Lord, and your demon hide belongs to me." With the edge of his sword, he sliced through the tentacles that had wrapped themselves around Leah's mind, then plunged the weapon directly into the darkest part of the demon's being. It immediately disappeared.

One of the other angels high-fived Leon. "Now that's how you slay a demon."

"Let's get to work," Leon said as he and the two angels dismissed all the demons that had been egging the situation on.

Now they had only one more to deal with. But he was the big daddy of them all, and he was hiding inside Ned. They would have to find a way to get him out, and then they would slay him, too.

21

"Take me to the Atlantis, please," Cory told the cabbie as he gingerly lowered himself into the backseat of a taxi.

About ten minutes into the drive, the cab swerved off the road and into a small ditch, tossing Cory painfully from side to side, even though he was wearing a seat belt.

"What in the world?" he muttered. Then, pressing one hand to his rib cage, he got out of the car to survey the damage.

"Tire went out," the cabbie yelled to him from the other side of the cab.

Cory went around and gazed in despair at the shredded rubber.

"I just bought that one," the cabbie said. "No way it should have blown out like that."

Cory turned to him. "Do you have a spare?"

"Yeah." The cabbie opened his trunk and retrieved the spare, along with a jack. He rested the new tire against the side of the car, then bent over to remove the spent tire.

The next thing Cory knew, the spare was rolling down the hill, picking up speed as it went.

He shouted to alert the cab driver. "Well?" he said. "Aren't you going after it?"

The cabbie scratched his head. "You're crazy if you think I'd ever catch it."

Cory could see the resort looming in the distance. He figured he'd be able to walk there before this cabbie got his act together. "How far on foot to the Atlantis?"

"About a mile and a half from here."

"I'm going to walk it. Good luck with your tire situation."

"What about my fare?" the cabbie asked.

Cory handed him a few bills. "That's all you're getting," he told him. "Next time, make sure you aren't rolling on worn-out treads."

***

As Cory headed down the street, Stephen left his post atop the hood of the taxi cab and continued fighting off the demons in pursuit of him. He had his hands full and was thankful that the people of God were praying.

⌒

"What's taking so long getting answers on my money?" Ned yelled into the phone.

"I'm working as fast as I can," Jonathan assured him, his voice projected over the speaker. "I'll call you as soon as I know something."

"Your job isn't to 'know something'—it's to make something happen, for your sister's sake."

"How is Leah?" Jonathan asked.

"She's getting on my last nerve. So, if you know what's good for you, you just might want to get me that money quick and fast." Ned hung up, then turned to Leah, whose mouth he had taped shut again. "Can you believe it? I don't think that brother-in-law of yours cares whether you live or die. I should have just kidnapped his wife. Nobody would want her dead."

Leah made a noise, so Ned yanked the tape off her mouth.

"Nobody wants me dead, either," she told him. "My family loves me."

"Yeah? Well, I sure can't tell."

"What happened to you, Ned?" she asked him. "What made you become so evil?"

Ned started strutting around the room as if he were the king of the world. "Didn't nothing happen to me. Nobody is dumb enough to mess with me, because I always find a way to win."

"Oh, right. Like the way you're winning right now, stealing from Jonathan? You probably don't even need his money; you just want to punish him for firing you. But I'm praying to God that your wicked plan for my family will not prevail. You don't have dominion over us. We belong to the Most High, and He will take care of us." She looked him up and down, not trying to hide her disgust.

He walked back over to the bed and squeezed her cheeks with his thumb and index finger. "Keep talking, and I'll show you how much pain I can inflict on you." Then his hand traveled down the length of her body.

Leah squirmed, trying to get away from his prying fingers. "Don't touch me. Don't you ever put your hands on me again."

"And what if I want to touch you all day long? You belong to me; I can do whatever I want to you."

"Untie me, and I'll show you what I'll do about it."

He laughed in her face. "I can hardly believe that you're the same girl who used to cower at the very sight of me."

She was about to respond to that when the door burst open, and Cory hollered her name.

Oh, no. Oh God, don't let this be happening. "Run, Cory!" she shouted. "Get out of here!"

"Where are you, Leah?" Cory called out, his voice getting louder as he came nearer.

"Don't come back here," she warned him. "Run!"

"Looks like I'm killing two birds with one stone today," Ned said, picking up his gun. "Tell me God isn't on my side." Then he left the bedroom.

Leah watched in terror as Ned lifted his gun and aimed it at Cory's chest. "Thanks for joining the party," he said. "You saved me the trouble of going to the hospital to finish you off."

Ignoring the barrel trained on his chest, Cory craned his neck to see around Ned. "Leah, are you okay?"

"She's better than you are," Ned said as he pulled the trigger.

The impact of the bullet lifted Cory off the ground and flung him against the back of the sofa.

Leah was nearly hyperventilating as Ned ran back into the bedroom and untied her from the bedpost. "Come on," he said. "We've got to get out of here before someone calls the police."

As he dragged her through the lounge area, Leah wept uncontrollably at the sight of Cory stretched out on the floor. His eyelids were fluttering open and closed. It was like the scene after the hit-and-run all over again.

"Don't die, Cory," she pleaded. "Don't leave me."

"Y-you're okay," he wheezed before his eyes closed and didn't open again.

"Nooo!" she screamed. "Why did you come after me, Cory? Why didn't you just wait at the hospital?"

"Come on," Ned growled. "Let's go."

"I'm not going anywhere with you," she spat.

"I'll put a bullet between his eyes if you don't come with me and stop that crying right now."

Leah believed that Ned would do just what he said. She couldn't let him shoot Cory again. She was still holding out hope that Cory would survive this blow. But if Ned shot him again, it would be over, and Leah wouldn't be able to live with herself.

As Ned dragged her toward the door, she pleaded, "Let me just call an ambulance for him, and I promise, I'll go with you. Wherever you want to go."

"There's my obedient pup," Ned said with a smile. "But I'm not calling an ambulance."

"He'll die if you don't!"

"That's exactly what I want him to do...die. Now, come on." He grabbed her arm and pulled her out into the hallway.

⌒

The Davisons arrived at the Atlantis at two in the afternoon. They went straight to the police and informed them that their daughter had last been seen at the resort and that they had received a phone call from her kidnapper that very morning.

"Did the kidnapper tell you that he was calling from the Atlantis?" Detective Drake asked them.

"No," David said, "but Leah has a room there. We were hoping that you would be able to take us out there and enlist the help of the hotel staff in searching the premises for her."

"Things don't work that way in the Bahamas," the detective explained. "You can't just show up here and claim that we've got some kind of kidnapping scheme going on. The Bahamians are, by and large, law-abiding citizens. They aren't interested in getting anything from tourists that isn't freely given."

"I think you misunderstood," Alma jumped in. "We are not accusing a Bahamian of kidnapping our daughter. We know the man who called, trying to extort money. Our daughter used to date him."

"Love gone bad, eh?"

"It started out bad," David corrected him. "Love was never part of the equation."

Detective Drake appeared to be in thought for a few minutes. Finally, he said, "Okay. I'll help you. Let's get over to the Atlantis and rescue your daughter."

"Thank you so much," Alma said.

"Don't thank me yet," he told her. "We still don't know for sure that she is being held at the resort."

They piled into Detective Drake's car, and as they sped off, Alma put her hand in her husband's. "We're going to find her, David," she told him. "God is with us on this journey. I can feel it."

22

I know why you shot Cory," Leah told Ned as he pushed her down a service staircase, his gun pressed against her back. "I know what you've done, and I'm going to make sure you pay for all of it."

"Shut up and keep walking," Ned snarled.

"Where are we going?" she asked as they traversed a landing in between floors.

"Wipe those tears off your face," he responded, ignoring her question. "If you make any attempt to draw attention to us when we're out in public, I will shoot you on the spot." He tucked his gun inside his jacket pocket, keeping it trained on her.

She had to think of a way to get back to Cory, and she couldn't do that if she was dead. So, she blinked away her tears and tried pasting on a smile, as if this were just another ordinary day. Nothing to see here. The love of her life wasn't lying on the floor of her hotel suite, bleeding to death. She wasn't being led away against her will. At gunpoint.

"Come on," Ned said, shoving her out of a service door. "Let's go for a walk down the beach, like two lovebirds out for a stroll. You know, just the way you and Cory did earlier."

Jesus, I need You to show up for me. Lead me and guide me. Show me what to do, she silently prayed as they made their way down the beach.

She had the sudden urge to sing praises to God, like she had been doing earlier. Things had seemed to get worse the more she prayed and praised, but Leah was reminded of a Bible lesson from childhood—the one about Joshua fighting the battle of Jericho. The wall didn't come tumbling down the first time the Israelites walked around the city, nor the second time, the third, or the fourth. It wasn't until the seventh lap that God caused the walls to crumble and granted victory to the Israelites.

So, she started singing about Jesus, and she kept right on singing, no matter how agitated Ned became.

After several minutes, he grabbed her arm and turned her around to face him. "Why do you have to irritate me so much?"

"Why do you have to be so evil?" With that question, a thought came to her mind, and she asked another: "*Do* you have to be so evil?" Looking into his eyes, she saw pure darkness—darker than anything she'd seen when she'd dated him. She was beginning to understand what was going on. Stepping away from him, she shouted, "The blood of Jesus is against you. In Jesus' name, I call you out, right now!"

⟳

"How dare you call me out!"

Slithering out of Ned was one of the biggest, most elusive demons Leon had ever come into contact with. But he had put the words in

Leah's mouth to get this demon to show his face, so now he would have to get to work. Failure wasn't an option, because it would cost Leah her life.

"I'm over here, you gutless lizard," Leon goaded him. "Come terrorize me, instead."

The evil one slithered toward him. "Get a good look at her, Leon. This will be your last mission."

As Leon reached for his sword, the demon stretched out its tentacles and wrapped them around the warrior angel, squeezing the life out of him.

〜〜

Alma, David, and Detective Drake followed a female clerk from the registration desk to the original room where Leah had been staying.

The room was empty, but there were signs of a struggle. "Her kidnapper must have taken her from this room," Detective Drake remarked.

Alma bent down and picked up a small canister of pepper spray. She handed it to the detective. "This belongs to Leah. I bought it for her myself." She leaned her head against David's chest. "Our baby is really missing, David."

"And we are going to find her," he said, rubbing her back. "Don't lose the faith on me now."

Pulling herself together, Alma said, "You're right. We came here to take her home." She turned to the clerk. "Her boss's name is Dean Richards. Can you call his room to see if he knows anything about Leah's disappearance?"

The clerk used her in-house walkie-talkie to phone the front desk. After a short conversation, she turned to them and said, "Mr. Richards has already checked out. There are only two people from the Pro-Site party who haven't checked out: your daughter and Cory Parker. And there are actually two suites under Mr. Parker's name."

"Cory is a friend of Leah's," David told her. "Can you call his rooms next?"

The clerk contacted the front desk once again, and the call was put through to Cory's suite, but it just rang and rang. "He's not there." The outcome was the same at the second suite under his name.

David turned to Detective Drake. "Now what do we do?"

"I think we should check the suites that were reserved under Cory's name. Leah and Cory might both be in one of them, unable to answer the phone for some reason." He turned to the clerk. "Can you get us into Cory Parker's suites? If for no other reason, then to rule out that they're in there?"

The clerk nodded reluctantly.

"Okay, then. Let's go get the keys."

❧

While Leon was taking the beating of his life from this enemy of the Lord, he tried to focus on finding a way out. Leah was depending on him, and he couldn't let her down. He had never failed a charge he'd been assigned throughout the ages of history, and he wasn't about to start now.

❧

"Let me go, Ned," Leah pleaded, trying to wriggle free of his grasp. She'd thought that casting out the demonic presence would make a difference, but he seemed more determined than ever to keep her captive.

"You'll go once I get my money, and not a second before. Keep walking."

"But Cory will die if I don't get back to help him in time."

Grabbing her shoulders, Ned pulled her so close that their faces were only inches apart. "Don't you ever say his name to me again. And since you're too stupid to get it, let me explain something to you: You've wasted your love on a dead man." He shook her. "Do you get it now? He was supposed to die."

She wasn't as stupid as Ned seemed to think. She had been putting the pieces together and had made several attempts to talk to Cory about it. Just to be sure, she asked Ned, "So, when you said that you didn't come to my office to kill me, you were telling the truth?"

He nodded. "That's what I told you. And if you behave, I'll keep you with me. I just want the money your brother-in-law owes me."

"Jonathan doesn't owe you anything. You're a thief, and you always have been."

Ned slapped her across the face.

The impact sent her reeling. She fell on her backside in the sand. But she was smiling wickedly because, just before Ned had shoved her, she'd grabbed his gun out of his pocket, and now she was pointing it at him.

"I guess you think you're going to shoot me?" Ned asked, advancing on her.

⌒

"You will not torment Leah even one more day," Leon said as he took the demon by the throat and plunged his sword into the depth of him.

The demon sputtered and spat out venom as he decreased.

This one wasn't going easy. Too bad for him that the saints of God were still praying for Leah. They hadn't given up and simply gone about their business. Leon pulled the sword out of the demon and plunged it back into him once again. The second time did the trick. Instead of just diminishing in size, the demon vanished altogether.

One of Leon's wings had been slashed and now hung, tattered and loose, by a thread. He felt like passing out, but his charge was on the ground, struggling with Ned for possession of his gun. He limped over toward them.

***

"Let go of the gun, Leah," Ned growled.

"You let go," she said, refusing to give up.

As Ned struggled to get the gun from her, he put his finger on the trigger and then turned the gun toward Leah. She felt herself losing control of the weapon, but she wouldn't let it go. She wouldn't let him win like this.

Then the gun went off.

～

"I could get in a lot of trouble for this if Mr. Parker is in there and doesn't want to be disturbed," the clerk told Detective Drake and the Davisons as they stood in front of the door to one of the two suites under Cory's name.

"And if he's in there, gagged and tied up, needing our help? Then what?" Detective Drake asked her.

"Okay, okay. I'll open it. But if I lose my job, I'm filing a complaint against you," she said, pointing a finger at the lawman.

Once the door was open, David rushed in first. "Leah! Leah, are you in here?"

Alma gasped at the sight of Cory lying on the floor in a pool of blood. "David, look."

As Detective Drake checked on Cory, Alma and David searched the rest of the suite. As soon as they saw the ropes on the bed, they knew that Leah had been held hostage in that room.

"Oh, dear Lord, what has Ned done with my baby?" Alma wailed.

23

Ned felt like dead weight on top of her. Leah pushed him off her back. That's when she saw the blood oozing out of his chest. Scared out of her wits, she backed away from him. His eyes were open but void, distant.

Leah couldn't speak. She couldn't breathe. Had she just killed Ned?

"Help!" she shouted, finding her voice. "Somebody, help!"

There were dozens of people walking or jogging along the beach, but they all seemed oblivious to her plight.

Finally, two men approached. One held a cell phone to his ear, apparently talking to an emergency dispatcher. "Yes, a man has been shot…. No, he looks dead."

The other man helped Leah to her feet. "What happened?"

"He—he kidnapped me. He had a gun, we tussled, and the gun went off."

"The police will be here in a few minutes," he told her. "Just wait here with us."

"I've got to get back to the hotel," Leah told them. "He shot my friend. I have to check on him."

"The police will want to speak with you," the man with the cell phone said.

"My name is Leah Davison, and I'm staying at the Atlantis. Please, call the dispatcher again, and have an ambulance sent to the hotel." Then Leah took off running down the beach as if she had jet propellers attached to her legs. She was running so fast that she feared she would fall on her face and end up in the hospital along with Cory.

As she rounded a street corner, Leah saw the ambulance. She wondered how on earth they got to the hotel so fast. But she didn't care. She needed to direct them to Cory's suite so that they could get him to the hospital in time to save his life.

She approached the ambulance, waving and screaming. "Thank God! Thank God you're here." But when she looked inside the ambulance, she didn't see any medics. Where had they gone?

Leah raced inside the hotel. She stopped one of the desk clerks and frantically asked, "Where are the medics? I need them to go to Cory Parker's suite. He's been shot."

The woman raised her eyebrows. "Ms. Davison?"

How did she know? "Y-yes, I'm Leah." She pointed back toward the ambulance. "Where are the paramedics?" she asked again.

"They're tending to Mr. Parker right now. Your parents found him in his suite."

"My who?"

"Your parents. They came looking for you."

The woman's simple statement reminded Leah of the Bible story of the shepherd who would leave ninety-nine sheep to go look for the one little one that had somehow gotten lost. Her parents had always been a perfect representation of Christ to her. If it had not been for their guidance through the years, she never would have made it this far through this ordeal.

The elevator doors opened, and Leah swung around to see Cory being wheeled down the corridor on a stretcher.

"Cory!" she yelled, rushing over to him. He was as pale as a ghost. She grabbed his wrist and felt for a pulse. It was faint, but he had one. "Heal him, Lord, for my sake. Please heal him."

"We need to get him to the hospital, ma'am," one of the paramedics told her. "You'll have to let go."

But Leah couldn't let go. She was still praying for Cory as she felt herself being moved to the side. Someone pried her hands away, and she saw Cory being lifted into the ambulance. "Let me come with you. Please. I need to be with him."

"Don't worry, honey—we'll take you to the hospital."

At the sound of her father's voice, Leah spun around, fresh tears falling down her face. She ran to him and wrapped her arms around him. "Thank you for coming after me, Daddy." She stepped back and saw her mother. "You, too, Mama."

"Are you bleeding?" her mother asked, frantically looking her over.

Leah glanced down at her shirt. It was drenched in blood, but thank God it wasn't hers. She hugged her mother. "No, Mama. That isn't my blood. It's Ned's."

"Ned? Oh my gosh. Honey, are you okay?"

"I will be. But I have to get to the hospital to check on Cory."

"Your dad can drive," her mother said. "On the way there, I'll dig out a fresh shirt from my suitcase for you to wear."

"Not so fast."

The three of them turned to the man who'd just entered the hotel.

"Detective Drake?" Leah's father said.

"I've got a dead body on the beach that needs to be accounted for."

It took a few hours, but after Leah had relayed her account to the detective, she and her parents were allowed to go to the hospital to see how Cory was doing. When they got there, they learned that he had just come out of surgery, and the doctors had high hopes for a recovery. Leah could finally breathe easy.

Leah and her parents crashed on some sofas in the waiting room, where they spent the night, receiving periodic updates on Cory's condition. By morning, he had awakened and was asking to see her.

As Leah entered his room, tears sprang to her eyes at the sight of all the tubes hooked up to Cory, at all the bandages covering his body. But he was alive, and she would forever praise the Lord for that.

"Don't cry," Cory said, grinning up at her. "Except for some busted ribs and the bullet they pulled out of me, I'm doing just fine."

Leah shook her head. "This is no time for jokes. I could have lost you yesterday. I don't know what I would have done if you had died."

"You would have survived."

Leah wiped the tears from her face. "I thank God that I'll never know." She leaned over and kissed him softly on the lips. "I love you, Cory, and I need you in my life."

"I love you, too, babe. And I thank God for sending you back into my life. Now if I can just get you to stop hanging around dangerous characters, maybe I can date you without being run over or shot."

She laughed softly, then said, "I wish I could take the blame for getting you in these predicaments, but there's something you don't know. And you aren't going to like it. I've got a story to tell that will bring clarity to everything that has happened."

"What do you mean?"

"All in good time, my love. Just rest for now."

⌣

Cory stayed in the hospital for a week and a half. Leah refused to leave his side the entire time. Not wanting to return home without their baby girl, her parents decided to stay in the Bahamas, as well, for a second honeymoon, of sorts.

When Cory had recovered enough to travel, they all flew back to the States together. One week later, Cory called a private meeting with Dean.

"Everyone is so excited that you're back and can get to work on our IPO again," Dean said as he took a seat on the sofa in Cory's office.

"Everyone but you, right?" Cory asked, sitting at his desk across from his business partner and so-called friend.

"Me? I'm excited, of course. We're going to be ten times richer than we are now. Why wouldn't I be thrilled about that?"

"Because of the dirty deals you made with Ned Turner behind my back." Cory opened the file folder on his desk. "This first document that Leah questioned you about clearly shows that you refinanced our building. You wanted Ned as our financial guy because he helped you steal from me. The two of you took two million in equity out of this building." Cory pulled another paper out of the file. "And this document shows that we are now in default on that loan."

Dean held up his hands. "I can explain."

"Can you explain why you tried to have me killed over this? Because that's something I'm very interested in knowing."

"It wasn't my idea," Dean insisted. "When you got all excited about the IPO, I went to Ned and told him that something had to be done about the money. He claimed that if I invested in his scheme, I would get tenfold on the return, but he lost my money. So, he figured that killing you would be easier than paying off a two-million-dollar debt."

"So much for friendship, huh?"

"It's not like that. I didn't want you dead, Cory. But I didn't have the money to fix the problem I created. So, I started losing things on purpose, becoming even more disorganized. But you went out and hired someone to handle that problem." Dean gave him an apologetic look. "My hands were tied. I didn't want to go to jail."

"Speaking of jail, how did you weasel your way out of the rape charge against Leah?"

Dean put his hand over his face and rubbed back and forth. "Before Leah killed Ned, he helped me grease a few palms, and we fed them a story about Leah selling herself."

"Did you get all of that, Leah?" Cory yelled over his shoulder.

Stepping out of closet, Leah said, "I sure did."

Putting another document on the table, Cory handed Dean a pen. "As of this moment, I no longer have a business partner. When you sign this document, ceding to me ownership of all the programs you have created thus far, and relinquishing your share of ownership in the company, and then go quietly, I will give you ten million. If you refuse, I will have you arrested. Your choice."

"Some choice," Dean said sullenly. He grabbed the pen and signed the document.

"The personal effects in your office are being boxed up as we speak. I want you to leave this building immediately."

Dean opened his mouth to say something, but then he apparently thought better of it and excused himself from the room without a word.

Leah sat down next to Cory and took his hand in hers. "I know that wasn't easy for you."

"Actually, it was kind of fun."

"If you had so much fun, why did you give him so much money to go away? He doesn't deserve anything."

"If it wasn't for the initial public offering, I wouldn't have given him anything. But I can't afford a scandal at this point in the game."

Leah was so in love with this man. He was everything she'd ever desired. She didn't care about the money he was about to make. She would love him no matter what. Because, like God, Cory had first loved her.

She pulled him close, leaned into him, and pressed her mouth to his, kissing him with open abandon.

When they managed to pull themselves apart, Cory asked, "So, are we still on for church with your family on Sunday?"

"Of course." She nodded. "And my mom has invited you to dinner afterward, so you'd better be on your best behavior."

With a wide grin, he told her, "I'll be even better than that."

24

The choir was on point, as always, performing to the glory of God under the direction of Marla Williams, who was turning out to be a great fit for the church. The words of the old hymn "What a Friend We Have in Jesus" kept running through Leah's head long after the congregation had finished singing it.

Leah smiled at Cory, seated next to her. Then she turned to her other side and remarked to her mother, "This place is really jumping."

Her mother nodded, beaming. "I can almost see the Lord smiling as He sits on high, enthroned in the very praises that are drifting heavenward from here."

The thought of that made Leah smile, too. It made her feel good to know that the Lord took delight in their praises. Even though she knew she would never be able to repay her heavenly Father for all that He had done in her life, Leah wasn't going to stop trying.

After the praise and worship portion of the service, her father stepped behind the pulpit. He offered a quick word of prayer, then asked everyone to turn in their Bibles to the gospel of Matthew, chapter 18. He started reading, beginning with verse 21.

"'*Then came Peter to him, and said, Lord, how oft shall my brother sin against me, and I forgive him? till seven times? Jesus saith unto him, I say not unto thee, Until seven times: but, Until seventy times seven. Therefore is the kingdom of heaven likened unto a certain king, which would take account of his servants. And when he had begun to reckon, one was brought unto him, which owed him ten thousand talents. But forasmuch as he had not to pay, his lord commanded him to be sold, and his wife, and children, and all that he had, and payment to be made. The servant therefore fell down, and worshipped him, saying, Lord, have patience with me, and I will pay thee all. Then the lord of that servant was moved with compassion, and loosed him, and forgave him the debt. But the same servant went out, and found one of his fellowservants, which owed him an hundred pence: and he laid hands on him, and took him by the throat, saying, Pay me that thou owest. And his fellowservant fell down at his feet, and besought him, saying, Have patience with me, and I will pay thee all. And he would not: but went and cast him into prison, till he should pay the debt. So when his fellow servants saw what was done, they were very sorry, and came and told unto their lord all that was done. Then his lord, after that he had called him, said unto him, O thou wicked servant, I forgave thee all that debt, because thou desiredst me: shouldest not thou also have had compassion on thy fellowservant, even as I had pity on thee? And his lord was wroth, and delivered him to the tormentors, till he should pay all that was due unto him. So likewise shall my heavenly Father do also unto you, if ye from your hearts forgive not every one his brother their trespasses.'"*

Leah had been feeling really good, because the church service had been electrifying. But what her father had just read from the Bible had killed the mood for her. It was as if God was telling her to forgive Ned. But wasn't it too late, since he was dead?

Closing his Bible, her father looked out at the congregation. "When we gave our life to the Lord, we asked Him to forgive us of all our sins. And I can tell you that my sins were many. So, I was grateful beyond words when the Lord wiped my slate clean."

"Amen," shouted several dozen congregants.

"You know it."

"I was, too."

"But how many of us have decided that someone else has done us too much harm to be forgiven?" her father went on. "Remember, forgiveness is not for the other person; it's for you. When you forgive, you free yourself so that you can move on with your life as a happy and whole individual, ready to love and to be loved. But if you can't forgive, you will never experience all that God has for you."

Leah had known he was going to say that. She respected her father and believed that he was a true man of God, but there were some things that Bishop David Davison didn't understand. He had never been beaten and stalked by a madman. He had never desired to die after being tormented by people who thought they could do whatever they wanted to him.

Leah tried to sit there and soak up the message. She knew that God was speaking to her, trying to get her to do what would be best for her Christian walk. Leah understood all of that, but she just couldn't make her heart forgive. Not right now. Not when the pain Ned had inflicted was still so raw.

She quietly stood, exited the pew, and made her way up the aisle. She headed for the nearest women's restroom, where she spent several minutes crying and giving God every excuse she could come up with for not forgiving Ned.

When she was done with her pity party, Leah dried her eyes, dabbed a little foundation on her face to cover up the tear streaks, and then returned to the service. Her father was wrapping up his message as she sat down.

Cory put a hand over hers. "You alright?" he asked.

She nodded, not trusting her voice enough to speak her thoughts. Then Leah caught the look her mother was giving her. Leah could tell that nobody was buying her need for a bathroom break in the middle of the sermon. The Davison kids had been taught better than that. She just prayed that her mother would let it go. She wasn't ready to discuss her forgiveness issues.

Thankfully, by the time her father came down from the pulpit after the service, all her family members were so hungry that they just wanted to rush back to the house and fill their bellies.

They were especially keen on eating once they learned that Leah's mother had made her famous turkey meat loaf with mac and cheese, sautéed greens, and candied yams. They added a leaf to the dining room table to make it large enough to accommodate two guests: Cory, of course, and Marla Williams. Leah was tickled to see the gleam in her brother Adam's eye whenever he stole a glance at her.

"Let's dig in," Adam said once the serving dishes were on the table.

"Hold on there," Leah's father said. "We need to offer grace over all this wonderful food."

He grinned as Adam put down the pan of meat loaf and Solomon returned the big spoon to the bowl of mac and cheese. Then he folded his hands and bowed his head. "Dear Lord, I can see that my boys are hungry, so I'm going to make this quick today. Please bless this food and the beautiful hands that prepared it."

"Amen," Adam said as he reached for the meat loaf again.

"Now, Father," Leah's dad continued, while Adam retracted his hand, "this family is so grateful for all Your wondrous works. We're thankful, Father, and we will forever give You praise, even for mere food on the table. But, if it would not be too presumptuous, we would also like to thank You for life, health, and the strength to live our lives in a manner that glorifies You."

Several voices around the table shouted, "Amen!"

"Amen," Leah's father said with a chuckle. "*Now* we can eat. Somebody please send the meat loaf and mac and cheese my way."

"You're not right, you know that, don't you?" Solomon teased as he passed the mac and cheese.

"Oh, you know I'm just messing with you and your brother. Y'all go on and fill your plates."

"I was going to get my meat loaf first, anyway," Adam told him. "If I wait until this plate gets back to me, with all y'all hungry folks, who knows if there would even be any left?"

Leah was happy to see that Adam was once again in a playful mood. He actually looked like he was enjoying himself, for the first time in months. She wondered if her brother had been able to truly forgive her for the disgrace she'd brought upon him. She couldn't blame him if he never did, but she really hoped that he would.

As she entertained that thought, she realized that the way she was feeling was exactly what her father had preached about that morning. She wanted forgiveness from Adam for all the havoc her wrongdoings had wreaked upon his life, but she herself refused to forgive Ned for the wrong he had done to her. *Oh, God, what am I going to do about that?* she silently prayed.

Suddenly, she had to know whether her brother had forgiven her. He was seated next to her, so she leaned over and said quietly, "Can I speak with you in the family room for a moment?"

Adam looked from his sister to his plate. "Can't this wait until after dinner? All I've eaten today is an apple at breakfast."

"Please, Adam?" she persisted. "If you can wait on dinner for just a minute or two, I'd really like to speak with you now."

Adam winked as he stood up. "You better be glad you're my favorite sister."

"Hey," Tamara complained.

"You're my favorite sister, too, Tamara…and you too, Larissa," Adam told them before following Leah from the room.

"You seem to be in good spirits of late," Leah commented.

"I do, don't I?" Adam was grinning in a way she hadn't seen for a long time.

"I'm not going to keep you from your dinner," she assured him. "But after hearing Daddy's message this morning, I was convicted for refusing to forgive that monster Ned for what he did to me."

"Don't beat yourself up over that, Sis," Adam told her. "You went through a horrific experience. It takes time to heal from something like that."

Leah lifted her hand. "I'm not excusing myself. I just wanted to talk to you, because I believe what Daddy said about forgiveness—that it's for the benefit of the person who was wronged, because it frees him or her to live healthy and whole, without bitterness. I don't want anything to hold you back from living your life, so I wanted to ask you to please forgive me for the way I messed up your life. I am probably doomed to carry bitterness around with me for the rest of my life, but I don't want you to live that way because of any unforgiveness you might harbor toward me. I know how it feels to carry that load. It's so heavy, and some days, it really weighs me down."

"Sis, I'm going to tell you this one last time: I have already forgiven you. And anyway, it wasn't your fault that I had a child out of wedlock and kept it a secret. If I hadn't acted so foolishly, none of the things you blame yourself for would have ever happened."

"But—"

"No buts about it. And, just so you know, I love Winter, and I'm thankful to have her in my life. That girl is going to make something of herself, and she has you to thank for that."

Leah hadn't thought of it that way. But the truth was, Winter's mother had been a complete mess. She wasn't fit to raise a pet, let alone a human being. But now, Summer was getting her life together, and Adam was able to be there for Winter. He was even paying her college tuition. Without him, Winter wouldn't even be in college.

"Thanks for saying that, Adam."

"Sure. Now can I eat my food? Daddy is probably stealing all the meat loaf."

Giggling, Leah followed him back to the dining room.

When they had finished dinner, just before dessert was served, Cory stood up from his chair, got down on one knee, and said to Leah, "What are you doing for the next fifty years?"

She laughed. "I don't know, why?" Was he doing what she thought he was doing?

He took a small box out of his jacket pocket, and when he opened it, the brightness of a diamond ring shined throughout the room. "Because I want to marry you."

She shook her head. "My parents have already done forty years, practically standing on their heads. If you can't promise me sixty years, it's a no-go."

"Lady, I can promise you an eternity." He kissed her, then said, "Make my dreams come true, Leah. God brought you back into my life because you and I were meant to be together forever."

She loved that his dream was no longer singularly about this IPO and becoming richer than Bill Gates but that it now included her and their love. She could work with that.

"So, you're saying I'm kind of heaven sent?" She kissed him again. "When you put it that way, how could I say no? Of course, I will marry you."

25

Leah never imagined marrying the man of her dreams, and with a destination wedding, no less. Since they were so familiar with the Bahamas, they decided to get married there. When Pastor Albury learned that Leah and Cory were engaged, he insisted that they have the wedding ceremony at his church.

They had decided not to stay at the Atlantis because everyone thought that the painful memories associated with that place might be too much for Leah to deal with. So, Cory booked a block of rooms for the wedding party and their guests at the Grand Lucayan.

Leah loved everything about the place. The moment they arrived, a feeling of serenity washed over her like a gentle wave, washing away all the worries of the world.

But when they went to Pastor Albury's church for the wedding rehearsal, Leah started having second thoughts. It wasn't the church that bothered her; it was the church's proximity to the beach where she had shot Ned.

Marla was the first to notice Leah's wariness. The two women had become close friends over the past several months. Marla had excused Leah's inappropriately timed outburst of laughter from the first time she'd visited the Davisons, because she now understood the reason behind it. And Marla hadn't taken long to figure out that what Alma wants, Alma gets.

Leah's mother had wanted Marla to become the minister of music at the church, and Leah knew something else her mother wanted—but she wasn't going to interfere. She knew she'd only mess things up.

"What's wrong, Leah?" Marla asked her from her seat at the piano, where she'd been practicing the solo Leah had asked her to sing and play for the ceremony. "You look like you're ready to bolt."

"I do not," Leah insisted.

Marla stood up from the piano bench and walked over to her. "Yeah, you do. Was coming back to the Bahamas too much for you? I'm sure your family will understand if you tell them that you'd rather go back home and get married."

"It's not that," Leah said. She was about to say more, but then her parents walked in, with Cory not far behind them.

"There you are." Cory came up to her and gave her a kiss. "You took off so fast, I didn't know if you had gone into the church or if you were walking down the beach."

"I wanted to get inside so I could see the beautiful decorations before the rehearsal," she told him.

Cory looked around the sanctuary. It was decorated with their wedding theme of silver and fig, which, Leah had explained to Cory, was a cross between purple and fuchsia. "It's beautiful, babe."

"Do you really think so?" Leah asked. Then she frowned. "I'm not so sure. I might have made a mistake on the colors."

"Are you kidding?" her mother said as she and Leah's father walked up to them. "This place looks wonderful. I wouldn't change a thing."

Leah turned to her father. "What about you, Daddy? Do you think I made a mistake coming all the way to the Bahamas to get married? I mean, you have that great big church back home in Charlotte, and yet, here we are, having traveled all this way for a simple ceremony. That's crazy, right?" Leah started laughing, and before long, she was in hysterics.

Everyone was watching her nervously, but she found she couldn't stop.

"Is she having a panic attack?" Marla asked the group.

Cory grabbed hold of Leah and started for the door. "Can you all make sure everything is taken care of here?" he asked over his shoulder. "I think I need to talk to my bride."

"We'll take care of everything," Leah's mother assured him. "Don't worry about a thing in here. Just go somewhere and calm her down."

Once they were outside, walking down the beach, Cory said, "Now can you please tell me what's wrong?"

Leah took a few deep breaths, finally calming down. "What makes you think anything's wrong?"

Cory stopped walking, then turned to Leah, lifted her hands to his lips, and started kissing her fingertips, one at a time. "Because I know you, sweetheart. You haven't been yourself since we arrived in the Bahamas."

"It's not what you think," Leah said quickly, trying to reassure her man. "I'm not nervous about marrying you. I love you and want to be your wife more than anything else in the world."

"Then what is it?"

When she didn't answer, Cory gently ran the back of his hand down the side of her face. "The only way we're going to have a successful marriage is if we start our life together with no secrets. Don't shut me out, babe. I'm right here, and I'm not going anywhere, no matter what the problem is."

"But that's just it." Leah's eyes filled with unshed tears. "You won't be here for me if I don't fix this. My hard heart will eventually drive you away."

He frowned. "What are you talking about? You don't have a hard heart. You're the gentlest, most loving person I know."

She turned away from Cory, not wanting to see his face as she broke his heart. "I don't think I'm the right woman for you. We need to call off the wedding."

Cory reached for her, tried to draw her toward him. "I'm not calling off our wedding, Leah. What's gotten into you?"

Pulling away, she said, "Just leave me alone, Cory. I need a little time to myself." Then she took off running down the beach.

⌣

Cory wanted to chase after Leah and beg her to think about what she was doing and how her actions would affect them for the rest of their lives. But she'd asked him to give her a little time to herself, so he acquiesced, praying that a little time would prove long enough to heal the wound she still suffered.

Adam got out of the car that had just parked at the church and came over to Cory. "Was that Leah who just took off running?"

Cory's shoulders slumped. "She said she needs time to think."

"Think about what? Did your stock just plummet, and she's trying to figure out if she wants to live in poverty with you?"

"No, my stock didn't just plummet. And I don't think jokes are appropriate at a time like this."

Adam put an arm around Cory's shoulders. "You're right. I'm sorry about that. I guess I was cracking jokes because I know Leah truly loves you. She won't go far. Don't worry. I know she'll be back."

They went inside the church and joined the others who had gathered for the rehearsal. As they approached the group, Alma's eyes flickered with questions.

"Where's Leah?" Bishop Davison asked.

"She's out on the beach, taking some time for herself," Cory said, unable to keep his misery out of his tone.

"I could tell something was bothering her," Marla said as she stepped away from the piano.

"Cold feet," Alma said. "That's all it is. She'll be back in a minute, I'm sure."

But Cory shook his head. "She doesn't have cold feet. She told me herself that she wants to marry me more than anything. But she's worried that—these are her words, now—her 'hard heart' will ruin our marriage."

"What hard heart?" Tamara asked as she and Jonathan joined the group. "And where is Leah?"

"Leah is off on her own, trying to figure out what she wants," Cory said. "She thinks she has a hard heart, and I don't know what she's talking about." He sighed. "I told her that I don't know anybody who's gentler or more loving than she is, but she refuses to believe it. She has completely shut me out." He sat down in the front pew and hung his head.

Just then, Larissa and Solomon entered the sanctuary, along with Pastor Albury.

"I thought we were supposed to be rehearsing for a wedding," Solomon said. "Where's the bride?"

"She needed a little space," Alma told him. "But don't worry. She'll be back before you know it. In the meantime, we can go on and rehearse without her."

"How are we going to rehearse without the bride?" Cory asked, getting up from his seat. "Doesn't she need to see how everything is going to go? Approve of all the details?"

Alma walked over to him and put a hand on his shoulder. "Do you still want to marry Leah?"

Cory nodded. "More than anything."

"Then listen to what I'm telling you. The bride doesn't need to know anything that's going on in the sanctuary before she starts her procession up the aisle. So, let's all work on that, get it perfected for her, and then David will guide Leah right to you tomorrow. Okay?"

Cory couldn't help but be skeptical.

Then David stepped forward. "I agree with Alma that we should go ahead and rehearse without Leah. But before we do that, we need to pray. Something has driven her away from here, and if we all come together in prayer, I am confident that God will bring about a change in this hard heart that Leah believes herself to be carrying."

"She definitely doesn't have a hard heart," Cory remarked. He wasn't going to let anyone think badly of his bride, even if she thought badly of herself.

"I agree with you," David told Cory. "But she says she does, and we must take her at her word." He looked around at the others. "Now, I'm getting ready to pray. Won't you all join me?"

Adam raised his hand like a student in grade school.

"What is it, Son?"

"I've been standing here, mulling this over, and I think I know what's eating at Leah." He moved closer to the rest of his family, now gathered around the altar. "About six months ago"—he pointed at Cory—"the same day you proposed to Leah, Dad preached a message about forgiveness. That afternoon, Leah asked me to forgive her for bringing confusion into my life. But I told her that I had already forgiven her.

"Anyway, she said that the reason she was asking for forgiveness was because she wanted me to be able to live a life free of bitterness. She also told me that she still hadn't been able to forgive Ned, and that she would probably carry bitterness toward him for the rest of her life."

"I didn't even know that she was still thinking about that monster," Cory admitted. "I told her that I didn't want any secrets between us."

"I think we know exactly what to pray for," David said. He held his hands out to the sides, and the family linked together in a circle as they took their problems to the throne of grace.

⌣

The captain of the host had been summoned. He didn't waste time wondering why; he just left his host of angels and made his way to the

Holy Place. He opened the massive doors that were laden with gold and stood in the back. The voice of thunder and lightning was speaking, so there was no one milling about. No one left or entered this Most Holy Place unless commanded to do so. As the Lord sat on His throne, a multitude of praises went up: "Holy, holy, holy." And as the voices became thunderous, Aaron bowed down, joining in the praise. In this place, where God sits high and is lifted up, praises are sung to Him forever. His glory and love fill the atmosphere, and joy spreads throughout His heavenly court.

Thunder and lightning sparkled from the throne of grace once more, and then Michael's glorious nine-foot form stood. His colorful wings glistened as they flapped in the air. "Yes, my Lord," he said, taking the scrolls from the omnipotent hand that held them.

Michael's sword was longer and heavier than those of all the other angels. Jewels were embedded throughout the handle of this massive sword, symbolizing his many victories. And the belt where his sword was holstered sparkled with the gold of heaven.

Michael held out the scrolls to Aaron. "Here is your assignment."

Aaron took the scrolls. "Thank you for entrusting this mission to us," he told him. "We will get it done."

26

Leah was despondent as she shuffled down the beach. The water was clear and blue; the sun was warm as it beat down upon her face. Lovers strolled the beach, holding hands, while she cried her eyes out. Loving Cory as much as she did, Leah couldn't bear the thought that her own deep-rooted bitterness might someday be the thing that would bring about division in their home. It had taken her own mother almost thirty years to get over the bitterness she'd held against Solomon and the woman who had birthed him. Alma Davison was a wonderful wife and mother, but Leah would not pretend that she didn't know what the woman's bitterness had done to Solomon.

Leah was at a loss for how to make what she felt go away. She didn't mourn the death of Ned Turner, but some nights, she had nightmares—not about the shooting but about the events that had occurred in the hotel suite beforehand. Specifically, when Ned had asked her to forgive him, and she'd refused. She had been refusing that forgiveness every day since, even to a dead man. And now, knowing all she did about Ned's scheme to rip off Jonathan, she had all the more reason to hate Ned and never forgive him.

The man of her dreams was waiting for her, wondering what was wrong with her and why she wanted to call off their wedding. The way she saw it, if she couldn't bring herself to walk down that aisle tomorrow and marry Cory, then Ned was to blame. Why should she forgive him for ruining her life?

Leah was stopped in her tracks by an invisible barrier, almost as if she'd collided with a force field. But when she looked up, she saw the tall man she'd bumped into. "Excuse me," she told him. "I didn't see you there."

"You are too blame…no one else," he said before walking away.

"Geeze," Leah said, frowning to herself as she resumed walking. What had gotten that man so upset? And what did he mean by saying she was to blame, and no one else? Hadn't she already apologized for running into him?

As she continued to walk, Leah noticed that the beach was empty, and that she'd somehow returned to the Atlantis. She didn't understand; she had taken off walking in the opposite direction. Yet, here she was, standing in practically the same spot where Ned had been shot and had died.

The man she'd accidentally bumped into was now headed back in her direction. Fear gripped her heart as she worried that he might attack her or retaliate in some other way. Her mind said *Run*, but her feet were planted in the sand and wouldn't move on command.

When he reached her, he said once again, "You are to blame."

"I already apologized, mister," she told him. "But, in case you didn't hear me the first time, I'm sorry. I didn't mean to bump you like that."

"And what if I don't accept your apology?" the man asked.

"Well, you should." That was all Leah could come up with. She didn't understand what the big deal was.

"Why? Because you want my forgiveness, even though you deny forgiveness to others?"

Stepping back as fear jumped into her heart, she said, "Who are you? What do you want?"

In answer, he simply said, "Your family is praying, but it's time for you to do your part, Leah. Put the blame where it belongs."

Was this man telling her that she was at fault for the terrible things that had happened in her life? Leah wrapped her arms around her chest and turned away from him. Who was he to speak to her that way? He didn't know anything about her or her situation. She turned back to tell him just that, but he was gone.

That's when she realized that he hadn't meant she was to blame for what had happened to her, but rather for her reaction to it. The bitterness that she had allowed to take root in her heart was there all because she'd refused to forgive and move forward with her life.

Leah slumped down on the ground, her tears blending with the sand beneath her feet and making a puddle, as she opened her mouth and began to pray.

"Lord, I need You. I rededicated my life to You in a church not far from this spot. But I have been keeping a part of myself away from You—the part that reserved the right to hate Ned Turner. Even though I know that Your Word says that a double-minded man is unstable in all his ways, I still claimed to love You while hating someone else.

"But this hate, this bitterness—it's destroying me. It's taking from me the man I love. The man I desire to spend the rest of my life with. This isn't fair to him, and it isn't fair to me. Ned is dead and gone, so I desperately need You to fix my heart. Take away the pain that is causing me to hold on to so much bitterness.

"What he did to me was wrong, but what I'm doing to the ones I love—harboring bitterness against someone else, and consequently making them pay for another man's crime—is even worse. I don't want to be like this. Because I know that if I don't let this go, I will not only eventually hurt Cory, but I will also bring additional harm to my family, eventually. My natural inclination is to be bitter," she confessed, thinking of the way she'd treated Larissa while growing up, just because she'd resented that her cousin was granted the same privileges as she and Tamara—"but You can make me better. So, I'm calling on You, Lord Jesus, to change me, so that I will not wreak havoc in the lives of the ones I love. Make me new, Lord Jesus, and I will forever give You the praise. Amen."

⤳

"Well, that's it," Alma declared. "We've prayed and we've practiced, so it looks like we're ready for tomorrow."

"All we have to do now is find Leah and go out for the rehearsal dinner," Cory said glumly.

Joining in prayer with his new family had reignited his faith that Leah would come to her senses and that everything would turn out alright. But they had been at the church for hours, and she still hadn't returned.

"Why don't we each take a section of the beach and search for her?" David suggested. "She probably purchased a book and is stretched out somewhere reading, trying to calm her mind."

"No I'm not, Daddy."

Cory pivoted toward the direction of Leah's voice.

"I've been at the spot where Ned died, crying my eyes out, as I prayed for the strength to forgive that man." She was standing in the doorway, looking as if she'd been in the middle of a whirlwind. Her eyes were bloodshot, and her foundation had been completely washed away by the tears that had streaked down her face.

But she was still a beautiful sight to Cory. He rushed to her and wrapped her in his arms. "I'm so glad you came back. I was so worried."

"I was, too," she admitted. "But for different reasons." She held Cory's hands as she told him, "I never want to be a burden or a curse to you."

"And you never will be," he assured her.

"Let me finish, Cory." She hugged him again as she said, "I have been carrying around so much hatred for Ned that it was beginning to drown out the love I have for you. I couldn't marry you as long as my hate for someone was greater than my love for you."

Cory held her at arm's length and looked into her eyes. "I had no idea you felt that way." Now he was the one having second thoughts. Maybe Leah was right—maybe it wasn't time for them to get married. He didn't think their marriage would survive if her hatred of another man outweighed her love for him.

"But as I walked the beach," she continued, "God directed me right back to where I last saw Ned. And today, I was finally able to leave him there. I felt the power of God come so strongly over me as I prayed and prayed to be able to forgive that man. And, finally, I did."

A wave of relief and gratitude to God washed over Cory as Leah stepped away from him and approached Bishop Davison.

"Daddy, your message about forgiveness was so true. The moment I forgave Ned for all the horrible things he did to me and to our family… it was at that moment that I truly felt free to love."

The entire family started praising God for her deliverance. As they were doing that, Leah walked back over to Cory and told him, "I'm sorry for what I said earlier. I don't want to cancel our wedding. Will you please marry me and give me a reason to believe in happy endings?"

He grinned. "I was still planning to be right here first thing in the morning, with my tux on. We've rehearsed the wedding already, so we're all prepared."

Leah turned to her family with a frown. "Y'all practiced without me?"

"Since you ran off, we had no choice," Larissa told her with a grin.

"But…I need to know what's going to go on at my own wedding. Can we just run through everything again?"

"No!" the group shouted.

"We're starving," Adam informed her. "And you are not about to deprive us of our long-awaited and well-deserved rehearsal dinner."

Leah turned to Cory. "And you're okay with this?"

"Babe, dinner was planned for six. We need to get back to the hotel and change."

"But…" Leah tried again.

"Everything will be fine. All you have to do is come down that aisle and say 'I do.' Trust us, because while God was giving you the victory over Ned, once and for all, we had your back. Our wedding is going to be beautiful."

Leah looked thoughtful for a moment. "You're right," she acquiesced. "I'm not going to worry about how the wedding is going to turn out, because I'm in this for the marriage, and I now know that our marriage will be as wonderful as we make it."

⌒

A catered meal awaited the group at the hotel. Once they had changed into their evening attire—floor-length gowns for the women, black suits and ties for the men—they were ready to get the party started. And no one was more ready than Adam.

For weeks now, he had been planning to ask Marla out; he just hadn't summoned the nerve to do so. But he told himself that if Leah could find the courage to forgive the man who had attacked her and to move on with her life, then he could find the courage to move forward with the woman he believed to be perfect for him.

He knocked on the door of her hotel room, then stood back and waited for her to answer.

"I'm coming," she called, then opened the door seconds later. "Oh! Adam. Hi. I thought it would be Leah. She and Cory were going to stop here on their way to the ballroom to walk with me."

"I told them to go on," Adam said. "I wanted to take you myself."

She hesitated a moment. "Are you sure?"

"As sure as I've ever been. Marla, I would like to ask that you be my date to the wedding tomorrow, and then, when we get back home, I'd like to take you out again, if that's okay."

She smiled. "I'd like that very much." She closed the door, took his arm, and let him lead her to the ballroom.

Just outside the double doors, Adam stopped and turned to Marla. "I don't want there to be any misunderstandings between us, so if you're going to date me, you'll need to know that I have three children."

"I already know that."

"Yeah, but did you know that two of them are by my ex-wife, and that she is mentally unstable? I don't think she'll bother us, because she's been receiving help for her condition. But I just want to be up-front about what I'm dealing with."

"Thank you for telling me that," Marla said.

"So, will you still go out with me?" Adam held his breath, praying that she would be understanding and willing to work with him.

"I don't see why not," she told him with a smile. "Let's just take it one day at a time."

Adam planned to do exactly that. He was going to woo Marla with each passing day until he wasn't just dreaming of marrying her but was making that dream a reality.

⌒

"It's about time," Leah said to her mother as Adam and Marla walked into the ballroom arm in arm. "You sure called that one right."

"Of course I did," her mother told her. "Who do you think got you that interview with Cory in the first place?"

Leah stared at her. "You acted like you didn't even remember who Cory was."

Her mother merely gave her a mischievous smile.

Leah shook her head in disbelief. All this time, she'd thought that it was just a coincidence that she'd run into Cory again. She should have known that Alma Davison had her hands in the mix.

She leaned over and gave her mother a kiss on the cheek. "You did good, Mama."

"What did she do good with?" Cory asked.

Apparently, her husband-to-be was just as clueless as she had been. But Leah was thankful that she had a praying, meddling mother. Otherwise, she wouldn't have found the man who was perfect for her. "She helped me to realize that God truly does send people into our lives for a reason. He sent you to me, and I'm so thankful."

"And don't you ever forget it," Cory said, giving her a kiss. "Until tomorrow," he whispered in her ear.

Epilogue

Leah couldn't stop studying her reflection in the full-length mirror on the wall of the church bathroom. Her floor-length cream-colored wedding gown made her look more elegant than the Duchess of Cambridge on her wedding day. As a matter of fact, with the way Cory treated her, she felt as if she were marrying her Prince Charming.

Her mother walked into the room, saw her, and burst into tears. "You look so beautiful." She took Leah's arm and lifted it, twirling her around. "You are always stylish, but this gown is so elegant."

Hugging her mother, Leah said, "Thank you for saying that. The funny thing is, I never believed you when you said things like that before. But I believe it today. Letting go of all that bitterness I had been carrying around has helped to open my eyes. I now see myself as God sees me."

"I'm so happy for you, honey."

"And I'm so happy to be marrying Cory. You couldn't have picked a better mate for me."

Her mother chuckled. "So glad you approve of my choice. Your dad and I can't wait to welcome Cory into the family."

"Are you sure Daddy's not upset that he isn't officiating the ceremony?" Leah asked. She had been worried that the romanticizing she and Cory had done over this wedding might have offended her father—something she wouldn't want to do in a million years.

"Honey, no, don't even think that. Your father knows how special this place is to you and Cory. You both rededicated your lives to Christ in this church, so why not have Pastor Albury marry you?" She smiled as she added, "And I'm just grateful for the excuse to get your dad to take another vacation."

"Thanks for being so understanding, Mama. Cory and I really felt a connection with this place. The fact that Ned died here no longer bothers me. I feel at peace in this place."

"Then it's settled. Now, let's go get you married off."

⌣

Cory watched the flower girl—his little niece—saunter gracefully down the aisle, tossing a handful of rose petals with every step she took. Then his gaze swept over his groomsmen—Leah's brothers—standing with him, and then Leah's bridesmaids, all standing with their bouquets in hand.

As the bridal processional song began to play, Cory raised his head to look down the aisle and caught the loveliest vision in white that he'd ever seen. Leah's dress was silky and dangled all the way to the floor. She held on to her father's arm as she strode down the aisle, looking nervous and excited at the same time.

Cory found himself thinking back to the days when they were in youth group and high school together. From the first time he'd seen Leah, he'd known that she was the one for him. It had taken Leah a lot longer to figure that out. The path back to each other had been a rough one, but they had made it, and now, nothing would ever separate them again.

When Leah's father handed her off to Cory, he grabbed her hand and pulled her close. Pastor Albury cleared his throat as they stood before him. Then he opened his Bible and read a passage from the book of Genesis, followed by Proverbs 18:22: "*Whoso findeth a wife findeth a good thing, and obtaineth favour of the* LORD."

The preacher went on to encourage them about the benefits of marriage. Then he addressed the guests and asked, "Is there anyone here who knows of a reason these two should not be joined together?"

No one spoke out against Leah or Cory, so Pastor Albury returned his attention to Cory and said, "Repeat after me."

Cory held Leah's hand, looked her in the eyes, and waited for the opportunity to repeat his vows.

Following the pastor's lead, Cory said, "I, Cory Parker, take you, Leah Davison, to be my wedded wife." With that first statement, Cory felt as if his heart was about to explode with all the love he possessed for Leah.

He felt calmer as he continued repeating after the preacher.

"Now, here's the really important part," Pastor Albury said, just before he led Cory in a pledge of faithfulness to Leah.

As Cory repeated the words, Leah's eyes became moist. He wanted to wrap her in his arms and wipe each tear away.

Pastor Albury then turned to Leah and said, "Repeat these words after me: I, Leah Davison, take you, Cory Parker, to be my wedded husband."

"I, Leah Davison, take you, Cory Parker, to be my wedded husband."

Once the rest of her vows had been spoken, Pastor Albury told Cory that he could kiss his bride. Cory didn't need any more encouragement. He pulled Leah to him and went in like man who'd been in the desert dying of thirst. "That settles it," he told her as they came up for air. "You are mine forever now."

"I wouldn't have it any other way."

About the Author

Vanessa Miller is a best-selling author, playwright, and motivational speaker. Her stage productions include *Get You Some Business*, *Don't Turn Your Back on God*, and *Can't You Hear Them Crying*.

Vanessa has been writing since she was a young child. When she wasn't writing poetry, short stories, stage plays, and novels, reading great books consumed her free time. However, it wasn't until she committed her life to the Lord in 1994 that she realized all gifts and anointing come from God. She then set out to write redemption stories that glorified God.

Heaven Sent concludes Vanessa's third series with Whitaker House, My Soul to Keep, which also comprises *Feels like Heaven* and *Heaven on Earth.* Her previous series are Morrison Family Secrets, comprising *Heirs of Rebellion* and *The Preacher, the Politician, and the Playboy,* and Second Chance at Love, of which the first book, *Yesterday's Promise,* was number one on the Black Christian Book Club national best-sellers list in April 2010. It was followed by *A Love for Tomorrow* and *A Promise of Forever Love.* In addition, Vanessa has published two other series, Forsaken and Rain, as well as a stand-alone title, *Long Time Coming.* Her books have received positive reviews, won Best Christian Fiction Awards, and topped best-sellers lists, including *Essence.* Vanessa is the recipient of numerous awards, including the Best Christian Fiction Mahogany Award 2003 and the Red Rose Award for Excellence in Christian Fiction 2004, and she was nominated for the NAACP Image Award (Christian Fiction) 2004.

Vanessa is a dedicated Christian and a devoted mother. She graduated from Capital University in Columbus, Ohio, with a degree in organizational communication. In 2007, Vanessa was ordained by her church as an exhorter. Vanessa believes this was the right position for her because God has called her to exhort readers and to help them rediscover their places with the Lord.